Contracted to Mr. Collins

SJ. Turner

Copyright © 2020 SJ. Turner

All rights reserved. The characters and events portrayed in this book are fictitious. Any similarity to real persons, living or dead, is coincidental and not intended by the author.

No part of this publication may be reproduced, distributed, or transmitted in any form or by any means, including photocopying, recording, or other electronic or mechanical methods, without the prior written consent of the publisher, except in the case of brief quotations embodied in critical reviews and certain other noncommercial uses permitted by copyright law. For permission requests, contact the author by e-mail, "Attention: Permissions Request," to: sjauthor@sjturnerstories.com

Content Notice: This book contains explicit adult situations and the use of mature language and is intended for persons age 18+.

ISBN-10 : 1794565078
ISBN-13 : 978-1794565074

Cover design by: izii_designer

Contents

Title Page
Copyright
Prologue
Chapter 1 – The Interview   1
Chapter 2 — Lunch   22
Chapter 3 — Skinny Dippin'   41
Chapter 4 – Max   72
Chapter 5 – The Car   90
Chapter 6 – The Dirty Girl Scout   106
Chapter 7 — Surprise!   126
Chapter 8 – Jamaica   150
Chapter 9 – Quality Time   181
Chapter 10 – A Quick Turn of Events   202
Chapter 11 – Oh, Hell No!   226
I'd love to hear from you!   255
About The Author   257
The Collins Brothers Series   259

Prologue

Aiden isn't at all surprised when he pulls into his driveway and finds Max's hummer parked by the garage. Even though they're almost thirty years old, as identical twins, they still spend most of their spare time together.

He grabs his suit jacket that still bears the latte from his morning encounter with the young lady he can't seem to get out of his mind and heads inside. The smell of mesquite wafts through the air as he makes his way out to the patio. That's where he finds Max. He's dancing next to the barbeque in a pair of running shorts with a beer.

"Hey! What have I told you about wearing those damn shorts here?"

Max chucks his chin at him and smiles as he turns around, placing his hand on his rump. "Seriously? See the way these make my ass look?" Turning back to face him, he grabs hold of his noticeable bulge in the front and gives it a shake. "And this, women love this shit, bro."

Shaking his head, Aiden chuckles. "This isn't a strip club, Max."

He turns, fanning his arm out left to right. "I don't see any women here at the moment to appreciate it. There's just you and me."

Gulping his beer, Max draws his brows together and

points at him with his bottle. "Speaking of which. When are we going to do something about that? I thought you were going to start looking for Mrs. Right."

Tossing his ruined jacket on one of the chairs, Aiden walks behind the bar and pulls out a beer. He twists off the cap and flicks it at Max with a smile. "Why haven't *you* found her yet? In case you've missed it, I'm running a corporation. What is it you're doing again?" He holds his hand in the air and shakes his head at Max. "Oh, right. You're too busy playing the playboy while using my name and house to do it. So again, I ask. Why haven't YOU found us, Mrs. Right yet?"

Squinting, Max looks across the table at him as Aiden takes a seat. "Wait a minute now. I've given you an amazing catalogue of beautiful women and had you named as the most eligible bachelor." He nods with a smirk as he gets up to slather more sauce on the ribs. "Besides, I share the fine prospects that I bring back here with you. Don't I?"

The corner of Aiden's mouth lifts slightly as he holds his bottle out toward Max with a nod. "That you do." Drawing his brows together, he tilts his head in question. "Although you seem to forget one thing, I actually want a wife all to myself. It's you that has this crazy idea that we should share one. Remind me why that is."

"Oh, come on, Aiden. We've been over this a thousand times. You're too busy to keep a wife on your own. She'll get lonely and end up cheating on you. If she's smart enough to have a kid or two, she can take everything you own with her, including half the corporation. The only way to avoid that is to keep her happy while you're busy. That's where I come in. You just get her to sign a contract, you're good with those. Offer her a generous compensation package in exchange for a trial period, let's say six months. We can slowly reveal our plan as she settles into the relationship. It's really that simple." Max chucks his chin and points to the stain on Aiden's shirt. "What the hell is that on your shirt anyway?"

He looks down at the stain, and the image of the flustered young lady from this morning floods his mind. She looked so innocent, practically running with her portfolio tucked in her arms and that damn latte he wore in her hand. "Well, I guess you could say I had a run-in with a latte this morning."

"You drink lattes now?"

Closing his eyes, he can see her face drop with dread as she watches him wipe off his shirt. He smiles and shakes his head, trying to clear the image. "No, but a stunning young lady that was applying for the account executive position seems to like them. She ran into me in the lobby, literally, and introduced me to her latte," he says, fanning his hand over the stain.

"Stunning, huh?" Max gets up and flips the ribs he has slow roasting on the barbeque. "Would you say she's a Mrs. Right type of stunning?"

Aiden slugs back his beer and smirks. "Not likely. She seems like she might be a little sexually naive. Nothing like what we're looking for."

Grabbing another beer, Max sits down and rests his forearms on the table. "I'm okay with sexually naive. I love a good challenge. Besides, we can slowly introduce the idea. Why don't you let me sit in on the interview with you?"

"I haven't even said she would get an interview yet."

A slow smile works across Max's face. "Yeah, well, you know she will. Shit, I can tell you right now just from the look on your face that girl will make it back in for an interview with you. You'll make sure of it."

"Either way, she's not the one. We want someone that's open to trying new things, someone that has a high sex drive and doesn't mind having us both in bed with her on occasion. She has to be able to keep our twin secret and be my dedicated wife and not only for social purposes. It's going to be difficult to find someone who can be a wife to both of us like you're suggesting. Besides, this young lady is merely looking to acquire a job. Now forget I even mentioned her." Aiden waves his hand toward the barbeque. "How long before those ribs are ready? I'm starved."

Pursing his lips, Max nods. "Fine. I won't say another word about her, but if you do call her in for an interview, I'd like to sit in on it." He lifts the lid on the barbeque and runs his finger over one of the racks of ribs then stuffs it into his mouth to lick the sauce off with a smile. "I'd have to say they're done. They've been cooking for a couple of hours now."

He glances back at Aiden and waves his hand toward the house. "I picked up potato salad on my way over. It's in the fridge. Oh, and grab us some plates."

"Yeah, I just worked all day, but let me get them." Grabbing his suit jacket from the back of the chair beside him, he walks into the house, still cursing under his breath. Aiden hangs his jacket on the hook by the front door making a mental note to call the cleaners and heads for the fridge. As he leans in to grab the potato salad, his phone hits the floor, and his personal assistant's name, Natasha, appears on the screen. "Hmm, maybe that's a sign. I guess it couldn't hurt to look over her résumé."

Setting the salad on the counter, he picks up his phone and initiates the call.

'Natasha speaking.'

"Natasha, I brought in a résumé this morning from one of the candidates and left it on your desk. Did you get it?"

'Yes, Sir, I did. A Miss Rebecca D'Angelo. I just added it to the received pile a few minutes ago.'

Aiden runs his hand through his hair smiling at the sound of her name. "Rebecca. Wonderful. Could you send me a copy? I'd like to look it over."

'Sure. I'll send it over in a few minutes.'

"Thanks, Natasha."

Sliding his phone into the front pocket of his pants, he leans against the counter and runs his thumb across his bottom lip. He needs to think of a way to keep Max busy while he checks this girl out. The one thing is for certain, he wants to know more about this Rebecca D'Angelo. If he can get Max out of town for a few weeks, he can follow her around himself, see what her typical lifestyle is like.

Max leans in the backdoor, his big booming voice interrupting Aiden's thoughts. "Hey! You getting the plates or what?"

He quickly bounces off the counter and spins to grab the plates from the cupboard. "Yeah. I'm coming! I was speaking with Natasha."

He sets the plates down on the table by the barbeque and pats Max on the shoulder. "I'm going to need you to go check out the place in Seattle we talked about last week."

"What?! I thought you said you had decided doing business across the border was too much hassle," Max says, eyeing him suspiciously.

Spooning some potato salad onto his plate, he nods. "Yes, it's a bit of extra paperwork, but Natasha says we're getting a lot of requests from that area. That tells me it could be a worthwhile venture, but we'll need to open a new office out there. I can't be in two places at once. So, I'm going to need you to go find us a suitable office space and possibly hire a few people to get it going."

Lifting his eyes to stare at Aiden from under his brows, Max sets down his fork and reaches for his beer. "You want me to not only find an office but hire staff? Are you fucking serious?"

"Yes, I am. You know the type of structure we require, and Natasha will prescreen the candidates for you to hire. I'll have her line up some properties for you to look at, and she can arrange your flight and accommodations tomorrow." Aiden holds his beer up toward Max with a smile. "It's time you did something to earn that handsome paycheck you see every month."

Max leans back in his chair with a cocky grin. "Wow! You're really going to trust me with this."

Nodding, Aiden smiles and takes a drink of his beer. "Just don't jump on the first place that you see. Take your time and check out all the places Natasha lines up for you. It shouldn't take you any longer than a month, maybe two at the most."

Reaching across the table with his fist closed, he bumps it with Aiden's. "You got it, bro. When do I leave?"

"I can have Natasha set everything up for you to leave tomorrow evening. She'll call you with all the details as soon as she has it all set up." He stuffs a piece of rib in his mouth and moans. "Mmm, damn good ribs by-the-way."

When dinner is over, Max heads for home to prepare for his trip, and Aiden calls Natasha to have her set up his accommodations. He places an ad in the Seattle Times and sets up the company information with a Seattle employment agency. Whether he had planned on opening an office across the border or not, it's a venture that's about to take place. He needs some time to see what Rebecca D'Angelo is all about, and he can't do that with Max around. If he feels she's worth taking the chance on, he has no intention of sharing her.

Chapter 1 – The Interview

The alarm blasts the new Khalid & Normani song Love Lies, starting the countdown to Rebecca D'Angelo's third and final interview at Collins Enterprises. It's rather surprising that she even got invited to the 1st interview, after accidentally dumping her latte on the CEO. She's positive it ruined his crisp white shirt and Armani suit that day.

Unfortunately, she recalls that morning all too clearly. Rebecca had heard about the account executive position at Collins Enterprises from a friend only a few days prior. With a whopping $75,000 annual base salary up for grabs, she couldn't wait to apply. Her aspirations were soaring as she put together a stunning portfolio and an impressive résumé, then marched herself directly downtown to the enormous office building.

With zing in her step, she walked up to the building and read the notice posted on the front door:

DEADLINE - Résumés for the Account Executive position must be received no later than 10 am this morning.

Pulling out her phone, Rebecca checked the time. It was

already 9:51 am. Unsure of where she even needed to go, she began to panic. She pulled open the heavy glass door and darted directly toward the information desk. At first, Rebecca had no idea what she had even run into – it felt like a brick wall.

As she crashed to the floor and her latte and portfolio launched into the air, her only thought was how thankful she was that she had considered protecting her documents with a plastic case. However, that thought abruptly ended when a set of large hands wrapped around her arms, helping her to her feet, and a deep rumbling voice echoed above. "Jesus Christ! This is not a schoolyard, young lady!"

Looking up, she couldn't believe her eyes. His dark hair was combed back neatly on the top and trimmed into a flawlessly tapered fade on the sides to meet his designer stubbled beard. The most amazing electric blue eyes she had ever seen stood out like stars against a perfect bronze tan that one could only achieve from the warmth of the Caribbean sun. She could feel the power radiate off his 6' 4" GQ cover body as she watched him wipe her latte from his crisp white dress shirt and expensive Armani suit. There was no mistaking who this man was — Aiden Collins, CEO of Collins Enterprises. Instantly she understood how he earned his status as one of the hottest bachelors in the business sector.

With a trembling hand, she picked up her portfolio. "I'm so sorry. The deadline." She managed to spit out as she stood holding the cheap plastic case in front of her.

Pursing his lips, he narrowed his eyes at her and extracted the portfolio from her hand. "Yes. Well, I'll see that it gets in." Turning his back to her, he walked away without another word.

That's the other reason she's so nervous about today — Aiden Collins will be the one conducting her final interview. Yep. That means her fate at Collins Enterprises now lies solely in his hands. On the bright side, she's made it to the third interview regardless of the latte accident. That must say something. Right?

Nervously, she stares at her closet. Now for the big question — what will she wear? She's usually more of a tank top and shorts kind of girl. Still, she can hear her mother's words of wisdom echoing through her mind, 'Honey, you must always remember to dress for success.'

However, Rebecca is fully aware shorts, and a tank top will not get her the position she's hoping for. So, she pulls on a black pencil skirt and white chiffon blouse over a cream coloured tank top and spins in front of her full-length mirror. "Okay, I can live with this."

She combs her mousy blond hair into a high ponytail, adds a little liner and mascara, then shakes her head and frowns in frustration at her reflection. Reaching up, she pulls out the tie holding up her hair and lets it fall loose across her shoulders. "Ugh! Come on, Becca. Which will it be, up or down?"

Her roommate and best friend Emma steps up behind her, watching as she stands tilting her head this way and that, scrutinizing her look from every possible angle in the mirror. "You need to chill out, Becca. You look great. Very office-e." Backing up, she eyes Rebecca's outfit and scrunches up her face. "Well, as long as you're not planning on wearing that outfit to the bar tonight."

Rebecca puts her hand on her hip and narrows her eyes, drawing a giggle from Emma. "Oh, come on, I'm just joking. Wear what you want, but that outfit is not going to get you any hot dates." She waves her hand in the air as if to erase what she had just said. "Anyway, stop fussing. You're going to kill this interview."

Rebecca turns to face her, forcing a smile. "I'm not looking for any hot dates, but I promise I will change before I come to the bar tonight."

Glaring back into the mirror, she begins to pull her hair up for the 4th time this morning and drops her arms in frustration as she glances back at Em through the mirror. "Hey, Em. Thanks for having faith in me."

She turns, snatching up her portfolio and keys from the side table. "Okay. I gotta run, or I'll be late. Wish me luck."

"Hey, don't worry. You got this. Here, heads up!" She hollers, tossing Rebecca a banana. "At least eat something. You'll feel better. Oh, and for god sakes, make sure you skip the latte this morning!"

"Yeah, yeah!" she says, shutting the door.

Rebecca places her portfolio on the passenger seat of her old Mazda and starts the engine. As it sputters to life, she pulls her seatbelt across her chest and takes a quick look into the rearview mirror. Her eyes roam across her face, and for a brief moment, the image of her mother flashes before her. She smiles, raising her hand to her cheek as if to embrace the fond memory. "Wow. I guess dad's right. I do look like my mom."

Traffic is a little heavier than Rebecca had anticipated, but she's confident that she'll make it there in plenty of time. She makes a right hand turn into Collins Enterprises parking lot and parks at the rear in visitors parking. When she steps out of her car, Rebecca takes a minute to gaze up at the largest glass building in Victoria. It's stunning. She can't imagine what the view must be like peering out from the 32nd floor. Catching her reflection on her way inside, she stops to straighten her blouse and push back a stray strand of hair before opening the main doors to the impressive lobby.

A short, dignified man with graying hair standing behind the information desk greets her with a broad smile then asks for her name and who she'll be seeing. "I'm Rebecca D'Angelo. I have an appointment to meet with Mr. Collins at 11 am."

The older gentleman nods politely and picks up his

phone. "Welcome, Miss D'Angelo. Let me quickly call up and see if Mr. Collins is ready for you."

"Of course. Thank you."

Rebecca stands patiently waiting while he calls up to confirm her information with someone on the other end. Once he verifies her details, he hands her a visitor's pass and points toward the long corridor. "You'll need to follow the blue dots on the floor to the elevator. Then take it to the 32nd floor and be sure to check in with Natasha at the front desk. You can't miss her. She's the little red-headed beauty as soon as you get off the elevator."

Waving with a wide smile, Rebecca starts down the corridor following the blue dots. She can feel the butterflies taking flight as she presses the button for the 32nd floor. Taking a deep breath, she steps back as the doors slide closed. Startled by the sudden whoosh as it bounds upward, she grasps the rail and stares up at the numbers as they tick by.

29…30…31…32.

The bell dings, signalling she's reached her destination, and she watches as the doors slowly glide open to a breathtaking view of the city below. Completely lost to the sight before her, she almost doesn't hear Natasha's soft voice call out to her. "Can I help you, hun?"

Rebecca spins around to face the beautiful redhead, grasping at her purse strap to save it from hitting the floor. The gentleman at the information desk wasn't kidding. Natasha is absolutely stunning.

Turning around, her words seem rushed as she blurts out, "Oh, yes. I'm sorry. I'm Rebecca D'Angelo. I have an appointment to see Mr. Collins."

Giving her a bright smile, Natasha stands to greet her. "Of course, Miss D'Angelo. Mr. Collins has been expecting you." She points down the hall to the row of doors. "It's that second door there on your left. I've been advised to send you right in."

"Thank you." Rebecca clutches her portfolio tightly to her chest as she strides toward his door stopping in front to gaze up at the nameplate before entering.

Aiden Collins CEO

Standing there for a moment with her eyes closed, Rebecca recites a quick mental mantra, 'Please, let him have forgotten that I ruined his expensive suit.'

Natasha notices her hesitation and waves her forward with a flick of her hand. "It's okay, honey. Really. Go on in. He's been waiting for you."

Rebecca nods, pushing the door open and coming face to

face with the man who not so pleasantly wore her latte only a mere three weeks earlier.

"Ah, Miss D'Angelo. It's a pleasure to see you again. No latte this morning?" He asks, waving her in with a slight smirk. "Please. Have a seat."

"Thank you, Mr. Collins. I assure you, the pleasure is mine." She hands him her portfolio and takes a seat in front of his desk.

Note to self - Mental mantras officially suck balls!

Her nervousness takes over, and the next words come rushing out before she can stop them. "About the latte incident, Mr. Collins. I'm really sorry. I was rushing..."

Aiden raises his hand to stop her. "Relax, Rebecca. I wasn't trying to upset you. My intention was merely to try and break the ice."

He settles back in behind his desk and opens her portfolio, flipping through several pages before his eyes meet hers once again. "It is okay that I call you Rebecca, isn't it?" he asks as he closes her portfolio and leans back in his chair.

"Right. I mean, yes. Of course. That's fine," Rebecca says, fidgeting with a loose string on the cuff of her sleeve.

Shit! Calm down, Becca. He's just a damn man.

A very wealthy, very powerful and incredibly gorgeous man — but he's still just a man.

"Good, and I'd prefer it if you call me Aiden," he says, undoing the button on his suit jacket. "You seem rather nervous. Do I make you feel uneasy?"

Uneasy? Heck no.

You make my mind take mini-vacations, my heart race, and my panties wet.

But I won't be telling YOU that. Now, will I Mr. Collins.

She shakes her head, trying to sound confident. "No. No, I'm fine."

Aiden locks his fingers together and places his hands on his desk in front of him. "I don't want to beat around the bush with this. Rebecca, Mr. Bradley and I both agree you are the perfect candidate for the account executive position. We would like to bring you on board."

Rebecca tries to suppress the smile fighting to form, as she stares down at her fidgeting fingers, trying to collect herself and gives him a slight nod. "Thank you, Mr. Collins. I'm very pleased to hear that."

YES! Oh, hang on. Why am I sensing there's more?

Because there is.

That 'more' is quickly confirmed as he stands and walks around to the front of his desk and rests his bottom against it, leaving only inches between them. His cobalt blue eyes lock with hers as the slightest smile graces his lips. "Rebecca, I'd like to take you to lunch," he says with an air of certainty as he calmly leans forward and cups her chin in his hand. "And I thought we agreed you were going to call me Aiden."

Staring into her eyes, she's sure he can see the crimson flood her cheeks as he waits patiently for her response.

Trying so hard to sound confident, Rebecca is sorely disappointed when a barely audible tone leaves her lips. She looks up at him, a bit baffled. "Lunch?"

A smile broadens across his face as he slowly releases her chin. "Yes. I'm sure lattes are not your main diet. You do eat real food, don't you?"

Straightening in her chair with a nod, she fights the urge to run her hand over her chin, where his hand had just been. "Yes. Of course, I do."

"Great." Aiden stands confidently, refastening his suit coat and adjusts his sleeves. His gaze holds hers as he picks up the receiver and speaks abruptly to his receptionist. "Natasha, clear my afternoon." He holds his hand out to her with a smile. "Shall we?"

What-the-fuck just happened? Is he really taking me to lunch?

She attempts to compose herself, reaching for his outstretched hand and clutches her purse in the other. "Uh, sure. I guess lunch would be all right."

She glances down at their hands, as hers nestles into the palm of his. It's large but soft, definitely not a hand that has ever seen a hard day's work. That she's absolutely sure of.

"I'll grab your contract from Natasha on our way out, and you can look it over on our way. We can discuss the details during lunch." He opens the door and guides Rebecca through, stopping briefly at the reception desk. "Natasha, can you give me Miss D'Angelo's folder, please?"

The beautiful redhead quickly scurries to the cabinet behind her and hands him a manilla folder. "Here you go, Mr. Collins. I've cleared your afternoon as you've requested, Sir."

He takes it from her hands with a slight nod. "Thank you. Oh, and advise Mr. Bradley, I'll be in touch with him this evening regarding Miss D'Angelo." He places his hand on Rebecca's lower back, guiding her toward the elevator. "Now, what would you like to eat?"

With her mind still whirling from the sudden turn of events this morning, she looks up at him with a glazed-over expression. "I'm not overly picky. I'm sure whatever you choose will be fine."

"Wonderful." A smile graces his face as he pulls out his phone, and his thumbs start flying across the screen.

This is not the Aiden Collins she was prepared to meet today. The man she researched is a demanding hardass –

a prick, to say the least, he's a businessman who doesn't like human contact, rarely smiles and always gets what he wants. As far as she can tell, she's already got the job. She certainly doesn't want to tick him off now by demanding a special lunch.

She watches Aiden slide his phone back into the breast pocket of his suit coat and press the button for the elevator. As the doors slowly slide open, his hand once again comes to rest on her lower back. He raises his other hand and gestures toward the mirrored elevator car. "Beautiful ladies first."

Rebecca steps into the elevator, amazed that she can still feel the heat where his hand had sat on her lower back a few moments ago. Never has a man had such an effect on her.

Aiden follows her into the elevator and presses the button for the garage. Her eyes instantly snap up to meet his. "Oh, I'm not parked in the garage. I parked in visitors parking outback. Could you press the main level for me, please?"

"I see no purpose of taking two vehicles. We'll take my car, and I can bring you back here after lunch," he says, closing the topic with no room for debate.

Ah, there he is! There's that demanding Aiden Collins I've read about.

With no room for negotiation, she decides to ask about

lunch instead. "Where did you say we're going?"

For a brief moment, she could swear he looks uncomfortable as he shifts his weight and stares up at the floor numbers as they tick by. "Actually, I didn't. However, I thought I'd take you to La Brasserie de Gloutonnerie. Have you been there before?" he asks.

She shakes her head in disbelief and looks down at her office attire before she glances back up at him with concern. "No, I haven't, but that's one of the ritziest places in the city. I'm not sure I've dressed appropriately for such a place. I doubt I'll pass their dress code."

Before she can say anything more, the elevator doors open, and Aiden places his hand on her lower back once again to guide her out into the garage. Offering some reassurance, he leans down close to her ear. "You're fine. You look beautiful."

She can feel the fine hairs on her neck stand at attention as his warm breath hits her skin and wonders if he can hear her heart pounding out of her chest from his close proximity.

Aiden pushes a button on his key fob, and the lights begin to flash on the sleek black Mercedes directly ahead of them. He steps in front of her to open the passenger door, holding it open while he patiently waits for her to settle in before closing it softly and walking around to the driver's side. He slides the key into the ignition and pauses for a moment looking over at her with tight lips.

She can feel his stare, but before she can react, he leans over, grabbing the seatbelt and pulls it firmly across her lap and clicks it into place. "What you do in your own vehicle is your business Rebecca, but everyone buckles up in my car."

She forces a smile and places her purse on the floor at her feet. "I'm sorry. I usually do, I'm not sure where my head is at today."

Aiden glances over at her as the engine roars to life. "I wish you'd relax. I would never hurt you." He places the manilla folder in her lap. "Here are the contracts. You can have a look over them while I drive, and we can discuss any questions or concerns you may have during lunch."

Curious that he has said contracts insinuating there are more than one, she opens the folder and indeed finds two contracts. At first, she thinks nothing of it. Most companies create duplicate copies, one for the company and one for the employee. However, upon closer inspection, she realizes they are entirely different. The first is between 'Collins Enterprises and Rebecca D'Angelo' as it should be, but the second one is only between Aiden and herself. She turns to face him feeling a little confused. "I'm not sure I understand why I would require a separate contract between you and me."

Turning to face her, Aiden graces her once again with that seemingly ever-present but apparently never to surface smile that everyone speaks of. "Well, Rebecca. I have a second offer for you to consider before you make your final decision." His voice is calm and confident as his gaze moves back to the road ahead. "Why don't you read through both of them, and we can discuss any of your concerns over lunch."

Her mind giving way to confusion, she finds it difficult to peel her eyes from his beautifully sculpted face. When she's finally able to drag her focus back to the paper in her hand, that's between 'Aiden Collins and Rebecca D'Angelo,' she begins to read.

The initial statements are reasonably standard for a customary agreement. She certainly doesn't see anything that should be cause for alarm. It clearly states that she and Aiden will be entering into a consensual 30-day agreement that will commence upon signing of the contract, blah blah blah. However, when she turns to page 2, where the terms of the agreement are outlined, she feels herself begin to flush.

Paragraph 1 – Media

For the purpose of media engagement, Miss D'Angelo consents to be photographed exclusively alongside Mr. Collins as his girlfriend/date/lover during the above stated 30-day period. She agrees not to divulge any personal details of their intimate relations to any media source at any given time during or after the said period of this contract has expired.

Girlfriend?

Intimate encounters?

Paragraph 2 – Place of Residence

Miss D'Angelo will reside solely at Mr. Collins's place of residence for the entire 30-day duration, effective immediately upon signing of the said contract. A common sleeping chamber will be shared for the entire term. This is non-negotiable.

Well, there it is. I'd be sleeping with him?! There's obviously been a mistake. He must think I'm an escort, not an account executive.

Paragraph 3 - Intimacy

Miss D'Angelo must be responsive to any and all requests/advances made by Mr. Collins, including but not exclusive to kissing, intimate touching, and intercourse. Mr. Collins is prepared to take into consideration any exclusions requested by Miss D'Angelo on the backside of this sheet. Furthermore, intimacy must remain exclusive during this entire period.

Is this a joke? Could I even consider this?

Rebecca flips the sheet, quickly glancing at the list on the opposite side. At the top of the page in big, bold letters, she reads 'Check Strong No's Only.' The page looks similar to a multiple-choice test. There are two columns with checkboxes beside each item. At a quick glance of the headings, she sees oral, vibrators and nipple stimulation.

Well, that doesn't seem so bad — especially when referring to a man that looks like he just walked out of a GQ magazine.

Wait...

What the hell am I thinking?!

For a minute, I want to slap myself for even considering this, but I'm honestly torn. I seem to have a verbal tennis match going on in my head with a saint on one side and the devil on the other, fighting between desire and disgrace.

Flipping the sheet back over, she continues to read.

Paragraph 4 - Remuneration

The total remuneration of this agreement is $300,000 plus any required items or gifts that may be acquired during this period.

$150,000 is to be deposited into Miss D'Angelo's bank account immediately upon signing the said contract with the remaining sum of $150,000 to be deposited upon satisfactory completion of the 30-day term.

She will have an open account at Gucci, Blush Clothing Boutique and any other clothing/salon/jewellery store of her choosing within the Greater Victoria or Vancouver areas during the duration of the contract.

Holy shit! $300,000?! This must be a joke.

Noticing the car has come to a stop, she closes the folder and looks over at Aiden. Rebecca's unsure how long they've been parked or how long he's been staring at her so intently, but when their eyes meet, an electrical charge surges up her spine. She can feel her vocal cords tighten, and when she opens her mouth, nothing comes out. Aiden seems to read her like a billboard as his deep voice pierces the silence. "You look scared, Rebecca." His voice is low and calm, and oddly enough, the sound of it gently soothes her sudden panic.

Shaking her head, she tries to gain some clarity on the situation. She's going to need to ask a few questions before she can agree to any contract of this nature, no matter how tempting the financial gain may be.

Flexing her vocal cords, she gives her voice another try. "Um, I think shock is the more appropriate word for what I'm feeling. I'm honestly not sure if I understand what it is that you're asking of me."

Looking a little defeated, Aiden exhales wearily and gives her a nod. "I can understand that you may have some concerns. Not to worry, we can discuss them over lunch." He opens his door, ready to step out and stops to look back at her. "Stay put. I'll come around to get you."

Aiden steps out of the vehicle and walks around to her side. As he opens her door and extends his hand, flashes erupt around the car. Rebecca looks up at him and shakes her head, mouthing the word 'no' while holding her hands tight to her chest. A bright smile forms across his face, and he gives her a reassuring nod. "Trust me, Rebecca. It's okay. I had a feeling you may be a little timid, that's why I parked at the door. Just ignore them. They're always here. We'll go straight in."

When she refuses to take his hand, his tone deepens, and his face tightens with agitation. "Rebecca, the longer you take, the more photos they'll take. Now, take my hand and let's go inside."

Her meek and mild side has suddenly been lost somewhere behind the lens of a camera, and her eyes narrow as she gives him a stubborn glare. "You never mentioned there would be any media here! I haven't agreed to your damn contract yet."

His eyes now wide as he pleads with her once again, he extends his hand. "Rebecca, please. The door is less than 20 feet away. I'll do my best to shield you from the photographers."

"Fine!" She grabs hold of his hand and leaps out of the car, darting into the restaurant with him in tow.

Once they're safe inside the doors, Aiden drags her to a stop and pulls her tight to his chest. "Whoa! Calm down. Why are you so upset about the photographers?"

Her first instinct is to shove him away, but the goosebumps erupting over her skin as she smells his cologne, and the safety she feels while in his embrace say otherwise. Conflicted, she steps back to look into his eyes. Now with some distance between them, her anger begins to resurface. He has no right to put her in this position. "What if I disagree with your contract? Those pictures today, they do nothing more than label me as one of your playboy conquests. I've seen your Google photo album, Mr. Collins. Although it's quite an impressive spread, I don't care to be part of it."

A smirk forms on his lips as he brushes a stray hair back from her face. "Then sign the contract Rebecca. Instead of a conquest, you'll simply be my girlfriend. You've clearly read the articles. You must know I've never been seen with any woman more than once."

Anger flashes through her like a lightning bolt. Before she realizes what has happened – she punches him in the jaw. "You're an arrogant asshole!"

She cradles her hand to her chest as the pain shoots across her knuckles and watches as Aiden rubs his hand along his jaw, moving it from right to left. From the look on his face, it's quite evident that he's angry, but as soon as his eyes fall to her hand against her chest, his anger quickly disperses.

"Shit! Are you okay?" He reaches for her hand and gently examines it, lightly kissing her throbbing knuckles then smiles down at her. "At least it's not broken. We can always get some ice from the waiter if you need it." His tone softens as he pulls her back into his chest. "Look, I'm sorry, Rebecca. You had every right to hit me. I did deserve that. I'm used to dealing with a different breed of women. You are right about that. Please, forgive me."

She pulls out of his arms and looks up at him, still full of disdain. "Yes, you did deserve that. I don't care if you are Aiden fucking Collins," she says through clenched teeth as she turns to leave.

Aiden reaches for her arm, spinning her back to face him. "Look, I truly am sorry. Sometimes I don't think before I speak. Please. Forgive me. I'll take care of any photos that may have been taken. Let's go for lunch. I had the manager set up a table on the rooftop. There are no photographers up there, and we can talk privately about any other concerns you may have with the contract." His eyes wildly scan her face for a reaction before he slowly releases her, putting his hands up in front of him in defence. "Just lunch, and a private conversation. For the record, I've mentally noted – no more unannounced media. I promise."

As the fog begins to clear and the adrenaline subsides, it finally dawns on her –

Oh my god! I just punched Aiden Collins in the jaw! Holy shit!

Noticing his defensive stance, Rebecca shakes her head, giving him a slight smile. "I'm sorry. I shouldn't have punched you," she says meekly, somewhat returning to the young lady that walked into his office this morning. "I'm not sure what came over me."

He runs his hand over his jaw as the corner of his mouth lifts into a half-smile. "It's okay. I can honestly say I deserved that." He shakes his head, and she watches his upper body jerk with amusement as he laughs. "For a little lady, you certainly have quite the right hook. I'll definitely try to use a little more tact in the future."

Chapter 2 — Lunch

Rebecca bows her head slightly to hide the smile forming and her crimson cheeks and begins to follow him through the kitchen to the elevator. Aiden stops abruptly and leans in close to her ear. "I'm almost afraid to ask, but are you okay with rib-eye? I pre-ordered for us, but I can change the order before we go up to the rooftop if you'd prefer something else."

She can feel the smirk pulling at her lips and tucks her chin to her chest to conceal it as she shakes her head. "No, rib-eye is a wonderful choice. Thank you for asking."

As the elevator reaches the rooftop, the doors slide open, and a waiter in a tuxedo is standing on the other side with a wide smile. "Good afternoon, Mr. Collins." He bows his head slightly toward Rebecca. "Good afternoon, madam."

Aiden places his hand on her lower back, guiding her toward their table and addresses the waiter. "I've pre-ordered our meal with the chef. Can you let him know we're here?"

"Certainly, Sir." He pours them each a glass of champagne, then scurries off to inform the chef they've arrived.

Leaning back in her chair, Rebecca takes a moment to observe this man in front of her – the very same man that has requested 30 days of her life for a price. A very high price. For the life of her, she can't understand why. He is the epitome of masculinity. The aura of authority that ripples off this man is apparent. People seem to jump to attention when they're in his presence. They beg to be near him, to have his approval. She's sure he could have anyone he wanted. So why does he want her?

The moment the elevator door closes, and they are alone, she can feel his eyes focus on her as his deep voice grabs her attention. "So tell me, Rebecca. What concerns do you have with the contract?"

She takes a sip of her champagne and contemplates the contents of the contract once again. "Well, honestly, it's the whole thing. Are you asking me to be your live-in sex toy for the next 30 days? Because if so, I'm afraid you have the wrong lady, Mr. Collins. I'm not an escort."

Aiden nearly chokes on his champagne as he tries to digest what she has just said. Straight-faced, he sets his glass down and glances up at her wiping his mouth with his napkin. "Not at all, Rebecca. I never once considered you an escort, and that is certainly not what I'm asking for unless, of course, you're offering. I have no problem adjusting the contract, and for god's sake, I thought we agreed you'd call me Aiden!"

Rebecca's mouth falls open, and her eyes grow wide as a sly smile works across his face. "Look, let's be honest. I could hire an escort for far less then I'm offering you for 30 days of your undivided attention. So please, don't devalue yourself or insult me with such nonsense."

"But you want my sexual preferences, and it clearly says I'd be sharing your bed," her voice rings with annoyance.

"Hang on," he says, shaking his head as he leans back in his chair, turning his spoon over in his fingers. "Let me try to be as transparent as I can. I'm 29 years old, Rebecca. It's time for me to settle down." Briefly glancing up at her, he raises his brow. "You're a smart young lady. I know you've done your homework just as well as I have. Can you picture the type of women that are in my phonebook?" She scrunches up her nose and looks down at her glass to avoid his gaze. "Exactly. Not quite the type of women you'd consider an honest relationship with."

He shrugs nonchalantly. "I'm rather drawn to you. I guess one could say you've awakened some part of my inner senses." His hand stills on his spoon, and he sets it down and reaches for his glass. "I find you very attractive and naturally wholesome. I've personally been observing you since the day you brought your portfolio into my office, and I very much like what I have seen."

Rebecca glares at him as a sick feeling washes over her.

"Wait! You've been stalking me?!" She's about ready to leave when Aiden's big hand reaches across the table and rests on hers. It brings an instant calm that settles over her, and she feels her body begin to relax.

His eyes soften as he holds her hand in place. "No. I wouldn't exactly call it stalking, more like observing. Besides, it's not uncommon for us to check out anyone we're considering bringing on board. We do it for two reasons. One, some people live double lives of illicit drugs and violence that we simply can't have associated with Collins Enterprises. Two, some are thieves and even reporters looking for the inside story. We have to be careful."

Aiden releases her hands as the waiter brings out their food, and with an annoyed look, he addresses the waiter. "Thank you. Could you please ensure that we're not disturbed any further?"

"Of course, Sir. There's a doorbell beside the door. Just ring if you require anything." Giving them a slight bow, he walks off, leaving them to their dinner.

Rebecca looks at her empty champagne glass and decides to pour herself another glass to accompany her dinner. However, when she reaches for the bottle, Aiden's hand covers hers. "Please, allow me." His radiant blue eyes twinkle in the afternoon sun as they meet hers, and he takes the bottle from her hand with a smile. "Now, as I was trying to explain. The contract is merely an outline of our relationship expectations."

Relationship?

She raises her brow, shaking her head. "Wait, is this your way of asking me to date you, because this is not the typical way it's done in my world, Aiden?"

He shrugs with an uncommitted nod. "Yes. Well, per se."

This can't be real! I'm about ready to start looking for hidden cameras or someone to jump out telling me I've been punked. He's either an excellent actor, or he's serious.

Setting his fork down across his plate, Aiden places his hands on the table in front of him. Intertwining his fingers together, he looks over at her. "Rebecca, the contract is simply to ensure both of our needs are satisfied. Think of it as a prenuptial of sorts. Just without the nuptials."

Her jaw drops, and she glances around the rooftop. "What?! This is a joke, right? Is someone going to come out now and yell, Gotcha?"

Shaking his head, he reaches for her hands once again and holds them snugly in his. "No, Rebecca. This is not a joke. Look, think of it as a trial period. You know, to see if I can live with you if you can live with me. To see if we can compromise, work things out together." He locks his pleading blues with hers and asks, "You wouldn't buy a car without test driving it, would you?"

Her eyes grow wide, and she can feel her face begin to burn. "Ugh! Seriously?!" she huffs. "You did not just compare dating me to buying a damn car?!" Still seething, she tries to pull free of his hands only to have him tighten his grip.

His eyes narrow, giving his head a slight shake. "Oh, no. There will be no more hitting," he says in a stern voice. "I apologize. I may have worded that wrong. I'm not very good at this sort of thing. I've never considered a relationship before I met you. What I mean is, we should be able to tell within the next 30 days if we are truly compatible for something more long-term." He carefully releases her hands and leans back in his chair, throwing his hands into the air in frustration. "This is not exactly going the way I'd expected it to."

"Oh, and what exactly did you expect, Aiden? Did you expect that I would just sign the contract, and we'd go back to your place to fuck like wild animals? I mean, this isn't exactly what I was expecting today, either."

Aiden's eyes now grow wide. This is not the wholesome young lady he's been observing for the past three weeks. He has unmistakably upset her. "Clearly, this is exactly why there's a need for a contract. The expectations are outlined, leaving no room for this kind of misconception." He downs his champagne and peers into her eyes. "Look, let me be completely honest with you. I have never had a real relationship before. I've never even considered one. Why Rebecca? — Because — I — know —

contracts. Not relationships! I have honestly never been with a woman for longer than a quick evening of mutual satisfaction in the past. Oh, and for the record, I hadn't planned on jumping straight into sex, but hell, if you're that damn adamant about it." He throws his hands up and leans back in his chair, shaking his head. "I'm certainly not going to say no. We can fuck like any damn animal you choose."

His outburst is purely out of frustration, that's clear and entirely out of character for the all mighty Aiden Collins, but it's kind of friggin' cute. She truly almost feels kind of bad for making him squirm a little. "Okay, okay. I'm sorry. I guess that may have been uncalled for." She takes his hand to offer some reassurance and to confirm that she understands the need for the contract on his behalf. "I just want to be sure I understand - the contract is merely stating that we'll be dating and that I can't tell the press about any of our intimate moments, is that right?"

A lopsided grin begins to form across his lips as his breathing regulates, and he contemplates his answer. "In a manner of speaking. Yes, that's correct."

The tension that releases from his shoulders as he says 'Yes' is almost palpable.

Ah, shit! He thinks he's just closed the deal.

Oh, you might be gorgeous, Mr. Collins, but I'm not quite that easy.

She tosses that statement around in her mind for a brief moment.

Oh, who the hell am I kidding?

I guess I am –

I don't need any damn contract to date him!

I have dreamt of having sex with him. Lots and lots of it!

I could care less if this only lasts for 30 days. I just don't want to seem too desperate.

Her mouth suddenly feels as dry as the Sahara desert. Rebecca reaches for her champagne, hoping merely to quench her thirst, but instead of a sip, she inadvertently gulps the remaining half glass. Rebecca calmly sets down her champagne flute, a bit stunned by her own actions and looks up at Aiden. As she squints against the afternoon sun, the lightning rod behind him causes her to take a second look - *Is that a Devil's pitchfork?*

Whoa!

Thankfully I'm not superstitious. Most would consider that a serious warning.

A giggle escapes her, and she throws her hand over her mouth in embarrassment. "God, I'm sorry. I think I've had enough champagne," she says, setting her glass back down.

The sound of Aiden's laugh is so sweet as it graces her ears. She can feel the tension at the table slowly dissipate. He waves off her apology. "Don't be silly. You're fine." Still smiling, he gestures to her plate. "Are you ready for dessert?"

"Actually, I could go for some Dippin' Dots ice cream from the harbour. I always have room for some of that."

A warm smile stretches across his face. "All right, I can make that happen. We just need to ring for the waiter."

Aiden takes her by the hand, and they walk over to the door to buzz the bell. It isn't more than a few minutes before the door springs open, and the waiter promptly steps through, looking a little surprised to see them both waiting by the door. "Is everything all right, Sir?"

"Oh, yes. Everything was perfect. Thank you. However, we've decided to skip dessert. My credit card is on file. Just charge our dinner, and be sure to add an appropriate tip for yourself."

"Thank you, Sir," the waiter replies with a quick bow. He holds the elevator door open, waiting for them to enter and gives them both a wide smile. "Thanks for dinning at La Brasserie de Gloutonnerie. I hope you enjoy the rest of your day."

"Thank you," Rebecca says as Aiden presses the button marked kitchen, and the elevator doors slide closed.

He steps back, resting against the rail beside her, and leans down to smell her hair. "I must say, Rebecca, you smell divine." A slight smirk emerges on his face as he straightens and watches the crimson fill her cheeks. It's difficult to believe this is the same little wildfire that punched him in the jaw only a couple of hours ago. When the elevator comes to a halt and the doors glide open, he extends his elbow to her. "Well, Miss D'Angelo, shall we go get some ice cream?"

Rebecca glances over at him and nods. "Absolutely, we shall, Mr. Collins."

Aiden guides her toward the back of the kitchen. "I thought you might prefer it if we snuck out the back door to avoid any photographers."

She smiles up at him with a nod as a warm feeling of appreciation flows through her. "I would prefer that. Thank you. I truly don't care to be seen within the pages of your portfolio." She looks up at him with an exaggerated smile and shakes her head. "I've never cared much for the media, and besides, I'm not a very photogenic person."

"Oh, I beg to differ, Rebecca. You're a lovely young lady," he says, setting his hand on hers as it rests in the crease of his arm and leading her out to the rear parking lot.

She's quite sure that her little scene out front had something to do with him having valet park his car in the rear. Still, she appreciates the gesture, even if it is because he doesn't want his reputation tarnished with photos of an unwilling young lady.

As they reach the rear parking lot, she takes a deep breath inhaling the refreshing ocean air from the harbour across the street. Rebecca has always loved the Inner Harbour, with its incredible gardens and statues, and this is the perfect time of day to go while it's busy with water taxis and sailboats. The walkway always has plenty of diverse entertainment with buskers from all over the world. She peers up at him with pleading eyes. "It's such a beautiful day, and the Inner Harbour is only across the street. Do you think we can walk across?"

"Of course we can. Just let me leave my jacket and tie in the car." Aiden undoes his jacket and tosses it in the backseat, then loosens his tie and pulls it over his head. Turning back to face her, he opens the top two buttons on his shirt and stills for a moment.

His eyes fix on hers. *That a girl, go ahead and have a good look at what I'm offering you.*

Rebecca stands admiring him for a brief moment as he discards his jacket and tie. She can't believe just how exquisite he really is. Her eyes slowly scan his body while her mind takes note of every visible feature.

Damn, look at how that crisp white shirt fits snugly over his broad shoulders. It's completely unable to mask the sculpted muscles of his chest and biceps as it tapers down to his trim waist. And that dark hair, I have an incredible urge to run my hand through those gorgeous dark locks that never seems to be out of place — and the need to feel that well-kept stubble that flawlessly graces his jawline. Is it really as soft as it looks?

Oh my god! He just licked his lips! Those full, and oh so sinfully tempting lips. I swear I just soaked my panties. Damn, what I would give to taste them. Oh, and those eyes, mesmerizing cobalt blue eyes that scream for attention.

Ah, shit!

Shit, shit, shit! Those beautiful blue eyes are staring back at me right now.

Smiling smugly as if he can read her thoughts, he holds out his hand to her. "Are you ready?"

Rebecca quickly blinks, taking a deep breath as she tries to suppress the crazy little twitch between her thighs. She squeezes her legs together and smiles. "Uh, yeah. I'm ready."

His eyes shift from her tightened thighs back up to meet hers as he tilts his head and raises a brow. "Do you need to use the restroom before we go?"

Crimson creeps across her cheeks as she grabs his arm with a giggle and tugs him forward. "No. I'm good. Let's go."

Casually strolling along the Causeway at the Inner Harbour, they stop every so often to hear a musician or watch an artist at work. When they finally reach the steps leading up to Belleville St., Rebecca spots the Dippin' Dots cart selling the best ice cream pellets ever made. They take their cups of tiny beaded ice cream treats and sit down on the grass overlooking the ocean.

As she lets the tiny beads of ice cream melt in her mouth, Rebecca starts to think about their lunch date.

All in all, if this were a 'real' date — it would be perfect. Almost. Minus the indecent proposal and the punch to the jaw. Oh, and I guess there's the whole comparing dating me to test driving a car.

Okay, never mind, maybe it's not such a perfect date after all.

She glances over at Aiden, who is propped up on his elbow, picking at the grass while he waits for her to finish her ice cream. She notices he seems to be a little agitated as he starts to pick small handfuls of the turf and toss them aside instead of single blades. He looks over at her and, like the true acquisition hunter that he is, squints his eyes in question. "Rebecca, I have to ask. Are you giving the contract any consideration?"

Her head falls to her shoulder, and she rolls her eyes. Swallowing what she has in her mouth, she clears her throat and looks at him out of the corner of her eye. "Aiden, do you honestly need an answer today? I'd like to have a better look at it before I commit myself." Finishing off her ice cream, she discards the dish in the trash beside her.

She watches him as he sits up, draping his arms across his knees and smiles at her. "I'm not surprised that you want a couple of days to think it over. In fact, I'd worry if you didn't."

He stands and brushes himself off. "Take a couple of days, that's completely fine. Today is Wednesday. Why don't we meet at my office Friday at 10 am? You can give me your answer then. How does that sound?"

If I could do it without drawing attention, I'd pat myself on the back. I've just entered the first phase of negotiations with Aiden Collins.

That's huge!

I've successfully stalled the King of Guaranteed 1st Proposal Closers.

She tries to keep her composure as she smiles ever so slightly. "Okay, that sounds fair."

Aiden laughs sardonically. "Yes. I have to say that's more than fair." Suddenly sounding all business again. "But I want you to know that I'll expect solid reasoning for anything you may disagree with. You see, Rebecca, I'm aware that my offer is quite generous. So, be sure you give it the consideration it deserves." He holds out his hand to her with a smile. "Come on. I'll take you back to get your car."

Once Rebecca settles into the passenger seat, she immediately goes back to examining the contracts. He's pleased that she's eager to get back to them, but it's probably best if she does that when she's at home on her own. He gently lays his hand over hers, closing the folder. "Why don't you go over them when you get home? My cell number is at the top. You can call me if you have any further questions or concerns."

Her smile is so sweet. It screams innocence as she shyly nods with a barely audible, "Okay."

Rebecca has her gaze fixed out the window as they drive back to the office, and it's that fortunate she does. Aiden seems to be too busy looking at her to notice he's missed their turn.

God, how many times in the last three weeks have I thought about those toned thighs wrapped around my head? Her ample breasts in my mouth –

"Um, Aiden. We just passed the office," she says, quietly drawing him back from his dirty little daydream.

"Shit!" He smiles over at her and pulls into the next driveway to turn around. "I'm not sure where my head is at today. It must be the distraction of your beauty."

He can't help but stare as she dips her head to try and hide the flush that works across her cheeks.

God, she's absolutely adorable.

Rebecca points toward the back of the parking lot, directing him toward her car. Sure enough, it's still parked in the exact place where he had seen it as they had driven by earlier. He looks at the offensive little car that should be in its new home at the scrapyard by now and cringes.

Jesus! I told Natasha to have that piece of shit towed. Obviously, they haven't gotten here yet. Now I'm going to need a new angle to be able to drive her home. I was hoping to be her chauffeur until I could convince her to sign the contract and get her a new car.

She points toward the old blue Mazda. "I'm the little blue one there at the back."

He glances at her as if she's crazy, slowing down alongside it, but he refuses to stop. "Rebecca, that car should not be on the road. When I saw it earlier, I messaged Natasha and asked her to have it towed. I thought someone left their scrap here. I'm surprised they haven't been by to pick it up yet." The look on her face is one of pure shock. For a moment, he wonders if he should protect his face from another fist. "Look, don't worry. I'll drive you home tonight, and I'll get you a new car in the morning."

Rebecca turns her head to look at him. She's so angry she can feel her eyes bulge. "What!? You knew that was my car! You've been bloody following me! You even told me so!"

He takes a deep breath placing his hands in the air defensively. "No. Well, yes — I did know it was your car, but it's not safe. Let's be honest. You don't need that specific car. You just need a car. That car is clearly a death trap Rebecca."

"You can't just buy me a new car. I haven't agreed to

either contract yet." Her glare slices through him like a scalpel as she balls her hands into fists and slams them down on her knees in frustration. "Aiden, stop! I'm not joking. Crappy or not, I need my car!"

He stops at the edge of the parking lot and turns to face her. "Look, I said I would buy you a new car – a safe car. I promise. No strings attached. You can consider it a gift. It'll be a tax write off for me."

She's so frustrated she flings her head back against the headrest and looks over at him. "Ugh! You cannot be serious? Do you have any idea how frustrating you can be? I'm supposed to be meeting my roommate Emma tonight at the Purple Lion at eight o'clock. I don't know anything about the buses in this city, and cabs cost a fortune."

Perfect! Another opportunity to spend some time with her.

He reaches for her hand and runs his thumb across the top, marvelling at the softness of her skin. "Rebecca, please, try and calm down. I will make sure you get there. I can pick you up at seven-thirty and take you myself."

Her head jolts up as she peers at him through wild eyes. "What?!"

"I said, I'll take you. You said the Purple Lion, right? I know where it is. That's no problem."

I've never been inside before, but I've followed her home from the place several times in the past three weeks.

She laughs, and it clearly has a cynical ring to it. "You are going to take me to the Purple Lion?" Aiden nods confidently. "You do know there are no crystal goblets or fine china there, right?"

He can't help but smirk at her thoughts of him. Sure he enjoys the finer things in life. Though when he's not in the public eye, he's actually quite down to earth.

I want so badly to show her the real Aiden Collins. The one that loves life, has a dangerous side and loves to break free from the suits and high society. The Aiden that wants to own her – body and mind. Even if it is only for a short time.

Rebecca clenches her teeth. He really doesn't seem to be getting it. She takes a deep breath and tries one last time. "Aiden, let me help you understand. People don't wear suits or drink champagne there!"

Ohh, she is a brazen little vixen.

Fighting to retain his composure, he raises his brow at her. "Rebecca, please. Will you trust me not to embarrass you? I'm trying to show you I can be accommodating and flexible. I'm not completely as I may seem on the exterior. You know, I do happen to own a pair of jeans and a t-shirt."

Deflating into her seat, she huffs exaggeratedly. "I'm not afraid you'll embarrass me. I just think it's completely out of your element, but if you feel you're up to it. I'll be ready for seven-thirty."

"Great!" He pulls into her driveway and shifts the car into park. Turning to face her with a wide smile, he reaches out to take her hand. "Then, I'll be back to pick you up at seven-thirty." He lifts her hand to his lips and lightly brushes a kiss over the very same knuckles that grazed his jaw earlier. "I only have one condition. You must promise there will be no more hitting."

She smirks then looks over at him with her brows drawn together. "I promise not to slug you if you promise not to treat me like one of your tramps."

A smile stretches across his face. *This girl is certainly nothing like the women he's dated in the past. She has her own mind and a feisty little spirit.* "Rebecca, I'm fully aware you're not a tramp. I promise to be on my best behaviour, and I expect that you will be too."

She purses her lips and gives him a slight nod. "Okay, then. I guess I'll see you at seven-thirty." Without another word, she steps out of the car and saunters up the walkway disappearing into the house.

Chapter 3 — Skinny Dippin'

It's already 6 pm when Aiden arrives home. He knows he still has a twenty-minute drive back to Rebecca's. So, he takes a quick shower and trims away any stray facial hair, then heads for his closet to find something to wear. He pulls on his favourite pair of distressed blue jeans, letting them ride low on his hips. Grabbing a new white Henley from the hanger, he pulls it on. He likes the feel. It's a bit snug, showing the defined muscles that lie underneath. He takes a quick look in the mirror, running his hands through his hair and lets it settle naturally. He splashes on some cologne and admires the laid-back casual look. It's just the right image he wants Rebecca to see tonight. She needs to see that he's more than just a tight-ass in a designer suit. Tonight, that small piece of the Aiden Collins he never shares with anyone is taking her out.

A quick glimpse at the clock tells him it's already 7:05 pm. "Shit!" Grabbing his keys, he heads for the door.

On his drive back to Rebecca's house, he fidgets with the radio, trying to decide what music he should have on. He puts on a country station then laughs to himself. 'I'm fairly certain she's not a country girl.' Flipping the channel again, he hears a familiar song by Leona Lewis and decides to leave it. He has a feeling they may enjoy the same taste in music.

He pulls into Rebecca's driveway and is quite pleased when he looks at the clock. It's seven-thirty on the button. Generally, he would bring flowers, but he doesn't want to push her. He wants her to believe he's doing this as a favour. He certainly doesn't want her to think he's considering this a date.

He steps out of his car, brushing his hands down his chest as though his shirt might wrinkle, then casually strolls up the walkway to her door and rings the doorbell.

When she opens the door, Aiden suddenly remembers why he's pursuing her while his brother's out of town. Max would be on her, like a fat kid on cake. He already regrets telling him about her at all.

Aiden takes a step back, letting his eyes roam the length of her body.

She's breathtakingly beautiful. Her blond hair is loosely draped over her shoulders, framing her oval-shaped face with soft subtle curls. Curls that he has dreamed of running his hands through almost nightly for the past three weeks.

The liner and mascara she's wearing gives her dark eyes a deep, sensual appeal that men crave, and lord knows he's definitely no exception.

The black spandex dress she's wearing has an open back and shows every contour of her body, leaving very little to the imagination as it hugs every curve perfectly. Ah, and she's wearing those signature black stilettos. God, how he's come to love those shoes. The way they lengthen her legs, making them scream for your attention.

Taking a deep breath, he tries to rein himself back in as he watches her take a casual glance down the length of him. Her eyes widen as she nods with approval. "Wow! I must say, I rather like the dressed-down Aiden."

He tucks his hand into the front pocket of his jeans with a slight smirk. "Well, thank you, Miss D'Angelo. You look rather stunning yourself." Raising his brow, he looks at her curiously. "I guess there's no chance you might have considered signing that contract while I've been gone. Hmm?"

She fumbles with the lock on the door, trying desperately to conceal her smile. "I thought we had agreed you were going to give me a couple of days to think it over. Friday morning was what we agreed to, wasn't it?"

"Yes, of course." Aiden places his arm around her and tucks her into his side with an adoring squeeze. "Of course, in my business, I've learned that the answer will always be no if you don't ask."

Aiden opens her car door and waits for her to settle in before shutting it and walking around to the driver's side. As he takes his seat, he looks over and admires the long locks that are draped over her shoulders. He can't resist the urge any longer. Raising his hand to her hair, he wraps a long tendril around his finger and closes his eyes, savouring the softness.

God, it's even softer then I had imagined.

"You have such beautiful hair, Rebecca. You should wear it down more often."

Heat quickly floods her cheeks, as she looks down into her lap, pretending to fidget with the hem of her dress. "Thanks," she says with a soft laugh. "You look like less of a tight-ass in jeans. You should try wearing them more often."

Aiden can't fully wrap his mind around this girl. The sound of sweet and sassy all wrapped up in one beautiful little bundle. He loves it. You never really know what side you're going to get. That sassy hot-headed side, or that meek, mild-mannered side. Nevertheless, this new double banger of sweet and sassy in one mouthful is making his manhood swell against his jeans. He's definitely going to need to keep Max away from her.

He shifts the car into gear, giving her a tight smile. "Thanks. I'll remember to keep that in mind."

They're almost halfway to the Purple Lion when the song Don't Matter by Akon comes on the radio. He hears Rebecca singing, and he glances over to see her head swaying in time to the rhythm and her finger tapping on her thigh. Pleased to see she's finally relaxed back into the young lady he's been observing these past few weeks. He turns his attention back to the road, tapping his fingers on the steering wheel to the beat with an inward smile.

The parking lot is full when they arrive, and Rebecca looks around a bit confused. "Hmm, that's odd. I wonder who's playing tonight. I don't recall ever seeing it this busy before."

Aiden pulls into the bistro parking lot across the road and looks over at her. "If we can't get in, I'd be happy to take you somewhere else. I mean, we're already out. I see no reason why we shouldn't enjoy our evening."

"Oh, I'm not worried about getting in. My roommate Emma works here. We'll get in." She points to the line-up outside the door. "Don't let that line-up bother you. We won't be standing in that."

Rebecca reaches for his hand, pulling him toward the door, but as they approach the edge of the parking lot - she freezes. Her face drops, and her breathing visibly increases. "Oh shit!" Her voice suddenly trails off to a weak mumble. "That's Alex Healey and the Mountain Vipers. Emma didn't tell me they were going to be here tonight."

"What's wrong? Are you alright?" Aiden asks, grabbing her by the shoulders and turning her to face him. "You look a little pale. If you're not comfortable being here, we don't have to stay."

She looks up at him nervously, her eyes almost pleading.

"Okay, Aiden. I'll spend the next 30 days with you like you've requested. I promise I'll sign the contract as soon as I get home."

"Whoa! Wait a minute. What have I missed?" This sudden shift has hit him off guard. He takes a step back to get a better look at her. As much as he wants to claim victory, he'd like to know what source is generating this rash decision. "Look, I'm ecstatic that you're suddenly willing to sign the contract, but it does raise the question of what it is that has caused this sudden change of heart?"

Stomping her foot in frustration, she looks up at him with tense determination. "Jesus, Aiden! Are you going to accept my verbal signature or not?"

Aiden stands back for a moment and contemplates her sudden change in demeanour.

Whoa!

Is she really trying to play hardball with me?

Me, Aiden Collins?

He runs his hand along the stubble on his chin, trying to contain his smile.

I kind of like this feisty side of her.

Hell yeah. We can play ball, Rebecca!

But, if we're going to play, we're going to play it my way.

Game on. Let's play ball!

"Rebecca, you know a verbal signature will never do. If you're serious…" He pulls out his phone, scanning through his files until he finds a copy of the contract and hands it to her. "Here. Just sign it."

He pulls his phone back briefly and reminds her that this is a real contract. "I want you to bear in mind that there is no turning back once it's signed. The terms of the contract will be effective immediately. You will leave here tonight with me."

It would be foolish to try to talk her out of signing it, but I'm not a total prick. I do want to be sure she understands the end result.

She bounces anxiously on the balls of her feet as she snatches the phone from his hand. "I'm not a child Aiden. I completely understand how contracts work."

His eyes widen, and he folds his arms with a smile as he watches her sign her name across his phone with a shaking hand.

Ah, yes. There it is. She's mine! All fucking mine!

She hands him back his phone with a sigh of relief that mystifies him. "There, now we're officially dating, right?"

Aiden's smile broadens. "Yes – Contractually speaking. It's official." He runs his hand through her hair. "Now, would you care to explain what caused your sudden change of heart?"

Shaking her head, she pulls him forward and continues toward the door. "I'm sure you'll understand soon enough."

As soon as the doorman Randy spots Rebecca, he gives her a wink. "Hey, Becca! You look hot." He studies Aiden for a brief minute then realizes who he is. "Oh, shit! Hey, Mr. Collins! Welcome to the Purple Lion!"

Aiden is still focused on Rebecca's sudden change of heart and the probability that someone at this club may have caused it. He gives him a quick nod, barely acknowledging him and protectively tucks her in close to his side. "Yeah, thanks."

Rebecca searches the crowd. "Hey, Randy. Have you seen Emma?"

"Sure, sweet thing. She's down at the back by the stage." He points toward the large table directly off to the side of the stage. Leaning in a little closer, he eyes Aiden skeptically. "Hey, um, Alex has been asking for you since he got here."

She nods, giving him a tight-lipped smile. "Thanks, Randy. I'll catch you later."

Alex, huh? He must be the reason for the sudden change of heart.

Gripping Aiden's hand, Rebecca strides toward the stage. The band is good. In fact, he recognizes them from the radio. He can certainly understand how they could draw a fair-sized crowd. Rebecca suddenly comes to a dead stop and is staring up at the stage. She has a glazed-over look. Maybe she's lost in the music or perhaps confused. He studies her for a few more seconds...

Shit!

She's not lost in the music,

and she's definitely not confused.

That's hurt.

Aiden steps up next to her and leans down to speak into her ear. "Rebecca, I'm not sure what the story is with you and that singer, but you can take refuge in me. Just tell me what you need."

As he steps back, she looks up at him, trying to blink away the tears that are beginning to pool in her eyes. "Kiss me. I just need you to kiss me."

Though he's a little taken back by her unexpected request, he doesn't hesitate to respond. Licking his lips, he slides his hand under her hair, gripping the nape of her neck and pulls her close. She melts in against him as her body begins to heat from his possessive touch. His mouth covers hers, and as his tongue slides past her lips, it seems to sweep away all her dilemmas. The tension that had consumed her body only moments ago slowly begins to subside. Breaking their kiss, he leans back slightly and lifts her chin with his finger to look into her eyes. "God, your lips are even sweeter then I had imagined."

Rebecca licks her lips and smiles up at him shyly. "To be honest. That kiss was exactly as I had imagined."

She turns toward the table where Emma is sitting and heads in her direction. If Aiden had to wager a guess, he'd say she's the one gawking at them with a gaping mouth and wide eyes flailing her arms in the air. "Well, this should be an interesting explanation," Rebecca says, shooting a glance in his direction. "I think I'm going to let you explain. After all, it was your idea to bring me here, and we're dating now."

As they approach the table, Emma stands to welcome them. She hugs Rebecca, then backs up and grasps her shoulders, keeping her at arm's length. A wide smile stretches across her face as she shakes her head. "Wow, Becca! I can't believe you brought Aiden fucking Collins to the Purple Lion!"

Smiling, Rebecca ignores her comment and pulls Aiden toward her. "Emma, this is Aiden Collins. Aiden, this is my roommate and best friend, Emma."

Emma flicks her finger back and forth between the two of them. Her eyes lock onto Rebecca's as her brow lifts in question. "Wait. Are you two on a date?"

Rebecca opens her mouth as if she's about to answer when Aiden takes a step closer and clears his throat. The corner of her mouth lifts into a slight smile as her gaze shifts back to Emma.

Oh, I can't wait to hear his answer.

He puts his arm around Rebecca, tucking her into his side and graces Emma with a huge smile. "Yes. I'm sure it all appears a bit odd, but I haven't been able to take my mind off of her since that first day we met in my lobby. We've spent our day together, and we've decided we're much more compatible on a personal level than a business one. Isn't that right, Rebecca?"

Quite stunned at how quickly he has spit that spiel out, she raises her brow and smiles up at him with a nod. "Mm-hmm. I couldn't have said it better myself."

She bounces up on her toes, kissing him lightly on his cheek to add some credibility to his explanation. "I would never have guessed it myself, but then here we are," she declares, snuggling into his side.

Emma's eyes meet Aiden's. "You mean since she dumped her latte all over you and ruined your Gucci suit," she says matter-of-factly.

The corner of Aiden's mouth lifts into a smile, and he dips his head with a nod. "Actually, it was an Armani, but yes.

That would be the day."

Still a bit skeptical, Emma's face slowly works into a smile as she sits back down, studying them both for a minute. Her eyes shift back to Aiden. "Well, shit! I kind of like you, Aiden." She gestures to the empty chairs on the opposite side of the table. "Well, what are you waiting for? Have a seat." Her eyes fix on Rebecca. "I'm not sure if you're going to like this, Becca, but Alex has been waiting to see you. He should be taking a break anytime now."

Rebecca takes a quick glance over at Aiden. "I'm not sure if we're going to stay. You didn't mention Alex was going to be here tonight."

Aiden places his arm across the back of her chair and twirls her hair with his finger. "The band sounds great. I see no reason why we can't stay for a bit. Why don't I go get us some drinks?" He leans his head against hers, letting his lips lightly brush against her ear as he speaks. "Look, you're mine now. I don't want you worrying about this guy. I won't tolerate anyone making you uncomfortable."

Rebecca gives him a nod and smiles. "You're right. I'd love a drink. How about something strong," she says with a wink as he gets up to leave for the bar.

Smiling down at her, he kisses the top of her head. "You got it. Don't go anywhere. I'll be right back."

As soon as Aiden leaves the table, Emma turns to her friend with wide questioning eyes. "Okay, Becca. What-the-fuck?! You have to tell me what I've missed before he gets back to this table. Do you want to explain to me how the hell you left for a job interview this morning then show up lip-locked with the CEO of the damn corporation?"

Rebecca's mouth hangs open slightly as she shakes her head, trying to think of what to say. Her hands go up as she shrugs. "It's just like Aiden said. We spent our day together, and I really like him. He's not the arrogant tight-ass I thought he was."

Aiden catches the tail end of their conversation as he returns to the table with a tray of drinks and can't help but smile. He's about to bring Emma's interrogation to an abrupt end. Nestling a shooter into Rebecca's hand, he raises his glass to hers. "I'd like to propose a toast. To us, new beginnings, and amazing discoveries," he says, clinking his glass with hers.

No sooner do they set their glasses down, and Alex's voice echoes over the noise of the crowd. "Ladies and gentlemen, we're gonna take a short break while we turn the stage over to DJ Slim for the next 20 minutes. We'll be back shortly. Don't go anywhere."

DJ Slim's voice ricochets through the room as a popular dance beat fills the air. When the band makes their way to the table, Alex glides up behind Rebecca. "Hey, Becca! Where's my hug? I've missed you, babe."

Her eyes briefly meet Aiden's, searching for reassurance before she turns to look up at Alex with a forced smile. "Hey Alex. How have you been?" She stands, giving him a quick hug, then swings around, gesturing to Aiden. "This is my…"

Before she can finish what she's saying, Alex finishes her introduction. "Aiden Collins, from Collins Enterprises, right? Yeah, I know who he is. Wow, nice to meet you, man." Shaking Aiden's hand, he looks back at Rebecca with a stoic mask in place. "I guess I should have called more. I'm really sorry, Bec. For what it's worth, I thought about you every day." He places a chaste kiss on her cheek and struggles to smile. "I hope you two are sticking around. When we go back up, we'll be performing a new single I wrote. It won't be officially released for a couple more days, but I'd really like you to hear it." He turns toward Aiden and pats him on the shoulder. "You're a lucky son of a bitch, Collins. She's one of a kind."

Aiden puts his arm around her and kisses her on the cheek. "You don't have to tell me. I recognized that the first day I met her."

Alex gives him a crooked smile and nods, hanging his head as he walks over to sit with Emma and the band.

Raising his brow at Rebecca, Aiden slides a shot glass toward her. "Here, I think maybe you could use this."

She doesn't even question what it is before she shoots it back. The burn is brutal as it slides down her throat, but she can also feel it numbing away the sting of seeing Alex. She sees a second shot glass sitting beside his arm and motions to it. "Do you mind?"

Shaking his head, Aiden hands her the shot glass and watches as she slams it back with a vengeance. He laughs as she shakes her head frantically, trying to calm the burn. "Are you okay now?"

She blows out through pursed lips, trying to cool the burn before plastering on a smile. "You know, I do actually feel a bit better."

He hands her the drink he's chosen for her. "Here, this is gin and tonic. I figured you'd need something refreshing after the something strong."

Taking a sip, she swirls the liquid around in her mouth for a brief minute. She nods with approval, then raises the glass and gulps it down. Setting the empty glass down on the table, she takes his hand. "Can you dance, old man?"

Can I dance?

Aiden fights to stifle his laugh.

She has no idea my twin brother Max and I paid my way

through college dancing.

"I might know a move or two," he says, letting her lead him on to the dance floor.

Rebecca is shocked as he starts to move around her to Please Me by Cardi B and Bruno Mars. Never in her wildest dreams did she imagine he was hiding those moves under his suit and tie. She's completely blown away when the music fades to Call out My Name by The Weeknd, and Aiden grabs her by the waist and turns her away from him. Pulling her back against his chest, he lays soft kisses along her neck while grinding his groin into her backside. The swell of his arousal pressing against her as they sway sets free a kaleidoscope of beautiful butterflies in her stomach. Her body begins to relax, forming to his as she fluently responds to his every movement. When she raises her head, she tenses. Aiden follows her gaze back to their table.

To Alex.

Ohh, fuck, no!

I'm not about to lose you now.

"Oh, no. No shutting down on me now, Rebecca." Turning her around to face him, he cups her face in his hands and lifts her lips to his. His tongue seeks out hers, and the passionate exchange is just enough to bring her focus back to him and the dance floor.

The microphone squeals as the music fades, and Alex's voice echoes through the speakers once again. "Thanks for sticking around. I have a new song I wrote for the love of my life." He chuckles softly, seemingly to himself, as he shakes his head. "Well, let's just say it's been a long road of should of's and could of's. Some may even say it's too little too late, but uh, here it is anyway. It's called Becca."

Rebecca sinks into Aiden's big chest as he wraps his arms around her waist and holds her close. "I'm guessing that's you, baby."

She nods, staring up at the stage. "Yeah, I guess it is, but like he just said – it's too little too late."

Aiden sways her in his arms as they watch Alex close his eyes and belt out a beautiful ballad. Alex finally opens his eyes and makes eye contact halfway through the song. He squints down at Aiden, then slides his gaze to Rebecca and winks. Aiden kisses her on the top of the head as a twinge of guilt passes through him.

Would her decision still have been the same if she had heard this song sooner?

When the song ends, they make their way back to the table, and Rebecca takes a seat on Aiden's lap. While toying with the back of Aiden's hair, Alex announces last call at the bar and says goodnight to the crowd. Between the tequila shooters and the gin and tonic, Rebecca definitely doesn't need anything more to drink. When Alex walks over and places his hand on her shoulder, the tiger that punched Aiden in the jaw earlier threatens to re-emerge. "Hey, Becca. Can I talk to you alone for a minute?"

Looking up, she tries to focus on his face, but her vision distorts, causing her to giggle. "Alex, I really don't feel I have anything to say to you. The song was lovely, but it must be for some other Becca you've been traipsing around with. 'Cause if you wrote it for me, you were right. It's too little, too late." Spinning back to face Aiden, she wraps her arms around his neck. "You should take me home. It might be the alcohol, but at this moment, I feel like I might punch him."

Aiden can't hide his amusement as he nods and lifts her into his arms. "I don't think she's in the mood to talk to you right now, Alex. Great show." His eyes fall back down to Rebecca, cradled in his arms. "I guess I better take her home. You're lucky. At least she gave you a warning." Before Alex can walk away, Aiden decides he'll pour a little salt on the wound for Rebecca's sake. "Hey, Alex. Would you mind letting Emma know she'll be staying at my place tonight?"

Alex sounds almost disconnected when he turns back to respond. "Yeah, sure. I'll let her know."

Rebecca tightens her grip around Aiden's neck and snuggles into his chest as they walk toward the door. "Thank you, Aiden. I couldn't have made it through tonight without you."

He sits her into the passenger seat and buckles her in, but as he's about to shut the door, she throws her arms back around his neck. "Wait, don't go. I love the feel of your arms around me."

A growl instinctively leaves his chest, and his manhood once again swells against his zipper. Kissing her, he calmly reminds himself they're in a public parking lot. "And I love holding you, but I can't hold you and drive." Unravelling her arms from his neck, he carefully closes her door and walks around to the driver's side.

Starting the engine, he leans his head against the headrest and looks over at her. Her head has flopped over to the side, and her hands are tucked together loosely in her lap. He can't believe he's finally taking her home with him. Of course, he didn't expect her to be passed out drunk on their first night together, but it has been an odd day for both of them.

They're not too far from his place when Rebecca starts kicking up a bit of a fuss. When he chances to look over at her, he sees she has unbuckled her seat-belt and is attempting to wiggle out of her dress. A little shocked by her actions, Aiden takes a deep breath. "Rebecca, what are you doing?"

She looks over at him with a frustrated pout. "Ugh! Aiden, it's so damn hot in here." He could turn on the air-conditioning, but he can't deny himself the guilty pleasure of watching her struggle out of that dress. When she can finally get it over her head, she tosses it into the backseat with a triumphant smile. Although Aiden loves the view, he's finding it more and more challenging to concentrate on the road as she sits there in nothing but a pair of skimpy panties and those sexy stilettos.

His erection is now at the full extent his jeans will allow, and he shifts to try and get comfortable. He takes a deep breath, breathing out slowly between pursed lips to try to regain some composure before looking back over at her. "You know, you could have asked me to turn on the air-conditioning."

Rebecca rolls her head to face him, her mouth agape. "You could have stopped me!"

"Yeah. I guess I could have," Aiden says, his eyes scanning over her bared flesh.

She relaxes into her seat and faces forward. "Meh, it's too late now. Besides, the leather feels cool against my skin."

Aiden pulls into his driveway and parks in front of the house. "Well, this is it. We're home."

She springs forward and gazes out the window at the huge house she could only dream of living in. "Are you shitting me? This is where you live?"

"Yes. I thought you did your homework," he says, getting out of the car with a sly smile. When he opens her door, she's still gazing up, and her eyes meet his. "I promise there are no photographers here, Rebecca. Now, would you like help to put your dress back on, or should I just carry you in as you are?"

The corner of her mouth lifts into a smile. "Well, if it's just us here and you've already seen me naked, I'd say there's no need to put my dress back on."

Aiden holds the back of his hand up to his lips, trying to hide his smirk and nods. "As you wish. I'll carry you in as you are."

As he bends down, she wraps her arms around his neck. "Hey, Aiden. I think I should tell you something, especially since we'll be living together for the next few weeks." Her words are coming out in a bit of a slur. "I really hate clothes. I have since I was a child."

He looks down at her with a wide smile. "You know, I can't say that disappoints me, Rebecca." Sliding his hand under her legs, he pulls her pliant body against him and lifts her into his arms. "Let's get you into bed. We can discuss your likes and dislikes tomorrow."

Kicking the car door shut, he turns toward the house with Rebecca giggling in his arms. Twisting her fingers through the top of his hair playfully, she says, "Aww, come on, Aiden. I'm not ready for bed yet."

Rolling her tighter against him so he can stretch out his

hand to punch his security code to unlock the door, he looks down at her and grins. "Oh, I think you are."

Rebecca huffs as they enter the house and begins to wiggle, trying to free herself from his arms. "Wow, this is a really nice house. Do you have a pool? You must have a pool," she says, craning her head to look around.

"Mmhm. I do." Rebecca twists so quickly he's unable to catch her before she launches herself from his arms.

Just barely landing on her feet, Aiden luckily catches her by the waist just before she topples over. "Whoa! You are quick, Mr. Collins," she says with a chuckle. "Lead me to your pool. Let's go skinny dipping!"

Okay, I told her I'm a gentleman and that I didn't expect sex right away. So, I'm going to give her a warning, but if she keeps persisting, then all bets are off. I mean, underneath all this calm – I'm still just a man. Watching her strip down in my car and those damn stilettos haven't helped the fact that I've been fighting a raging hard-on all night.

"Rebecca, I need to warn you. I'm not sure I'd be able to keep my hands off you if we go skinny dipping. In fact, I know I won't. We should probably get you a t-shirt and call it a night."

Standing in front of him in nothing but her panties, she runs her hands down his chest and sticks out her bottom lip in an exaggerated pout. "Aw, don't be a party-pooper, Aiden. I don't want a t-shirt. I want you to get undressed and take me to the pool. Your contract promised intimate moments, didn't it?"

Done!

All bets are officially off!

She has been warned. Yet she continues to tempt me.

I will be taking what's mine!

A low groan comes from his chest as he strips off his shirt, tossing it to the floor. Rebecca's shyness has been lost somewhere in a bottle of gin, and she's actively eye-fucking him as he unbuttons his jeans. He's so turned on by the sight of her biting her bottom lip in nothing but her panties. He lets his jeans drop to the floor and walks straight toward her. Standing toe-to-toe, Aiden tucks his finger into the waistband of her panties and licks his lips. "Are you sure you want to go to the pool? There's a king-size bed upstairs."

A slight flush works its way over her body, and he would put money on the fact it is not from embarrassment. Oh, no. It's from pure lustful need. "Mmm-hm. I'm sure," she says, taking his hand and letting him lead her through the house to the patio. With a flick of a switch, he turns the pool lights on, and her eyes light up with amazement. "Sweet!"

Aiden grabs two bottles of water and sets them down on the edge of the pool, then gestures toward the stairs.

"After you, pretty lady."

Without hesitation, she takes a few steps back and runs, leaping into the pool. When she breaches the surface, she tosses her panties at Aiden's feet with a giggle. "Okay, it's your turn!" she calls out with a mischievous grin. He's still trying to wrap his head around this brazen wild side of hers, but the vivid images of what will happen once he gets into that water begin to dance around in his mind. As the saliva starts to pool under his tongue, he swallows hard and meets her eyes with a cunning smile.

Aiden's boxers drop to the pool deck, and Rebecca's eyes grow wide as she watches him stride toward her. With his imagination still running rampant, he's done wasting time. Diving in, he swims up behind her and presses his naked body against her backside. His arms slink around her waist, and he pulls her tight against him. "God, Rebecca, I love the feel of your bared flesh next to mine." His hips jut forward, letting the evidence of his statement reveal itself against her bottom.

Turning in his arms, their lips meet as he guides her up against the wall of the pool. When her sinful tongue slips past his lips to play, he slides his hand down between their bodies and guides a finger inside her, coaxing out a slight moan. He quickly pulls back and gazes at her curiously.

He knows she's not like the women he typically dates, but still, at twenty-one, he didn't expect her body to be quite this snug. He hasn't witnessed her with another man in the past few weeks while he's been tailing her, but he's sure there's no way she's still a virgin.

Rebecca's eyes spring to his with a look of disappointment. "What's wrong? Why'd you stop?"

He looks into her eyes, "Rebecca, when's the last time you had sex?" Quickly, he raises his hands in defence. "It's just really snug down there. I don't want to hurt you. I need to know you're not still a virgin. I mean, if it's just that it's been a while, then I'll take my time, that's all."

Her mouth drops open, and she lets out an exaggerated huff. "Ugh! Really Aiden? You weren't concerned about the possibility of me being a virgin or the last time I had sex when you wanted me to sign your contract." Raising a brow, Aiden urges her to answer. "Fine! It's been a while!"

"How long exactly is a while, Rebecca?"

"Jesus, Aiden!" She glares at him, but his gaze remains unwavering as he waits for her response. "God! I was sixteen! Alex and I agreed we'd wait until our wedding night after that, but things didn't work out between us." She throws her hands up in frustration. "What does that even matter? I'm not a fucking virgin."

Taking a deep breath, he leans his forehead against her shoulder.

Holy fuck! Could I really be this blessed?

Lifting his head, he looks into her eyes. "Well, it's probably going to hurt a little. That's a long time, and you're pretty tight."

She gives him a devil-may-care smile and shrugs. "I'm sure you won't mind that it's tight, and at least this time, I've had some alcohol to ease the pain."

Locking her lips with his, she wraps her legs around his waist and wiggles her hips. Butterflies begin to swirl in her stomach as she feels the head of his dick firmly wedge against her opening. She grips his shoulders and rocks back and forth, slowly trying to manoeuvre him deeper into her entrance with each movement.

Aiden breaks their kiss and cups her face in his hands, fighting to make eye contact. His words come out in a forced breath. "God! Rebecca, let me take you inside where I can ease you into it. I don't want to hurt you."

He can see her need growing stronger by the minute. Her eyes widen as she tightens her grip on him. "No, Aiden. You wanted this! And trust me, at this moment, there's nothing that I want or need more. So just fucking do it!"

Her brazen words have him throbbing at her opening, and he's not about to argue with her.

He grabs her hips, stares deep into her eyes and repositions himself against her. "Fine, but this may hurt a little."

He gently begins to slide upward, inch by agonizing inch. Rebecca can't take it anymore. She abruptly digs her hands into his hair, grabbing a handful. Pulling him into her, she grits her teeth. "Don't go slow!"

Done!

With one quick thrust, he lets out a guttural moan feeling her warm body accept him.

Rebecca gasps, gripping onto his shoulders. Her muscles begin to contract around him, and she digs her nails deep into his flesh. "Shit!"

Still not completely penetrating her, Aiden does his best to try and stay still and allow her body to adjust around him. However, his natural instincts have him slowly rolling his hips. He brushes a strand of hair back from her face. "Are you okay? Do you want me to stop?"

Biting her lip, Rebecca shakes her head. "No. This isn't the kind of pain you think it is. My body is screaming for release," she says, her voice now raising an octave as she stares into his eyes. "I need to cum. Just do it, or I'll do it my damn self!"

Aiden can't help but smile at her words, he loves how she was holding this wild side so close to her chest, and he's all too eager to oblige. He pulls out slightly then pushes back in, gaining a little more depth with each stroke. "I promise I'll get you there, baby, but you really need to try and relax a little."

His thumb finds her swollen bud, and he begins to gently stroke, bringing her closer and closer to her release. Her head drops back, and she lets out a low moan. Her hips are now moving in time with his thumb, simultaneously working him deeper into her warm flesh.

Small waves of excitement flash through her stomach, and she can tell her orgasm is cresting. Aiden pushes in deeper, working his thumb across her now very swollen bud, and she lets out another moan. His own body is begging for release as much as hers, and it's all he can do not to let go when her body tenses and her muscles begin to tighten around him. "Oh – My – God! Yes, Aiden!

"That's it, Baby." As her orgasm rips through her, it drags him deeper and deeper into her with each throbbing pulse.

His gaze is focuses on her face. Watching her lose herself on him is—

So erotic.

So intense.

Her breath catches, coming out in short bursts as her thighs begin to tremble. Thankful that she's finally found her release and knowing he's not far behind her, he covers her mouth with his and grabs hold of her hips for leverage. As her muscles continue to contract around him, he thrusts forward and completely buries himself. A moan of pleasure roars from his chest. He's never felt anything like it. Her warm, soft flesh surrounds him like a pulsating vice.

He thrusts once.

Twice.

He holds himself deep inside her as his balls tighten and begin to tingle. Finally, his own anticipated release pulses through the head of his dick. "Ohhh - Fuck!"

His heart pounds out of his chest, and his breathing is erratic as he slows his thrusts to smooth, even strokes trying to bring himself back to the present.

Dropping his head to her shoulder, he takes a deep breath. "Jesus, you're amazing." He hasn't been this wound since he was a teenager. His body is still so tightly strung that his throat has momentarily constricted, causing his voice to come out as a deep growl.

Giving her a kiss, he reluctantly shifts out of her hold and slowly pulls away. "It would have been helpful if you'd have mentioned you hadn't had sex in the last five years," he says, wrapping a towel around his waist as he hands her a bottle of water.

"Would it have made a difference?" she asks, opening her water and taking a drink.

Aiden shrugs. "I wouldn't have let you talk me into

skinny dipping, that's for sure. It probably would have been a little more pleasant in a more controlled environment. You know, like a bed," he says with a smirk.

"I think you controlled our environment perfectly." She accepts his extended hand allowing him to help her out of the pool and settle her on his lap.

He drapes a towel across her hips and kisses her cheek. "All joking aside, is that why you panicked when you realized Alex was at the bar tonight? You didn't know how else to say no to your first love?"

"Yes. Well, no. It's more than that." She looks down at her lap, trying to hide her crimson cheeks and lowers her voice. "I couldn't bear the humiliation of him knowing I hadn't moved on yet. I mean, I have mentally. I don't want him anymore. I just haven't made an attempt to date anyone since he left." She looks back up at him. "And obviously, he's been with a ton of women since he left."

Not only since he left. Alex has always had a problem with being faithful. She's caught him cheating on her too many times to count. Somehow he's always had a way of convincing her it wasn't his fault or that it was all in her mind. Even when the evidence was glaring at her, she caved and gave him the benefit of the doubt – she loved him.

Realizing she used him to get back at her rockstar exboyfriend, he forces a smile and gives her a knowing nod.

Fair enough.

Whatever the reason, it just cost her the next 30 days at my whim.

With this new understanding, he cradles her into his arms and kisses her on the cheek. "Well, I'd say his loss is my gain. I'm certainly not going to dwell on it. Let's go get some sleep. We need to go find you a car in the morning, and it's already past three."

Lowering her onto the bed, he briefly hovers above her. "To be clear, Rebecca. With or without a contract, you're not some conquest as you may think." He kisses her softly and rolls onto the opposite side of the bed, pulling her against his chest.

Thoroughly sated, she smiles. "Thanks, Aiden. I needed to hear that."

Chapter 4 – Max

The next morning Rebecca's awakened by heavy banging on the bedroom door and a loud rumbling voice. "Come on, Aiden. Get your punk ass up! I know you're in there. Your car is in the driveway, and I just saw the panties of last night's victim out by the pool."

Releasing a groan into Rebecca's ear, Aiden pulls her tighter to his chest. "Just ignore him, he's an idiot. With any luck, he'll go away." Luckily, semi-conscious Rebecca realizes she's naked and reaches for the sheet just as the door bursts open. Aiden quickly flies up, ensuring she's covered and gives their intruder a mouthful. "What-the-fuck, Max?! You can't just come barging in here! Get out!"

Max laughs as he covers his mouth with his fist. "Oh shit, man! I'm really sorry." He throws his hand out toward Aiden in defence. "How was I supposed to know you'd have a chick in here? Since when do you let chicks spend the night?"

Rebecca takes a second glance at Aiden's double standing by the door. She covers her reddening face with the sheet while trying to melt into Aiden's chest as best as she can.

He has a freaking twin?! Why didn't I know about this? I've researched this man and his company inside and out!

Keeping a protective arm tightly across her chest, Aiden lifts himself onto his elbow to finish dishing it to Max. "Since I've started dating someone! Now watch your mouth, and remember this is my fucking house." He cranes his neck to look at the alarm clock beside the bed and shakes his head. "What are you doing here, anyway? Do you realize it's eight o'clock in the morning? Besides, I thought you were going to be in Seattle for another month."

"I called the office, and Natasha said you took the next month off. Being your caring older brother, I thought I'd make sure you were okay." Max gestures to Rebecca on the bed then quickly pulls his fist to his lips, trying to conceal his smile. "But now, I'm starting to understand why. Aren't you at least going to introduce us?"

"Knock off the older brother bullshit. It's two fucking minutes, Max!" Aiden uncovers Rebecca's face keeping his arm tight across her chest. "Rebecca, in case you haven't put the pieces together yet – I have a twin brother. Let me rephrase that. I have a loud-mouth twin brother," he says, glaring up at Max. "Rebecca, meet Max."

"It's nice to meet you, Becca," Max says, leaning down with his hand extended.

Aiden quickly smacks it away. "Fuck off, man! What are

you thinking? She's obviously not dressed!"

"Alright, alright!" Max laughs, putting his hand up in front of him. "I'll wait downstairs, but hurry up." He looks back to Rebecca and shakes his head. "Damn, girl! You must be something pretty special to spend the night in the playboy's forbidden den," he says, before stalking out of the room and slamming the door behind him.

Aiden gazes down at her with an awkward smile. "I'm sorry. He was supposed to be in Seattle."

His lips meet hers, briefly igniting a memory of the best sex she's ever had. "Mmm. Good morning," she says, pulling him down for another kiss.

"Rebecca, I would love to spend the day in bed doing unspeakable things to you. However, now that Max knows you're here, he won't let up until we go downstairs. Not to mention, I promised we'd go find you a car today. Remember?"

"Uh, Aiden. There's one small problem." She sits up, holding the sheet tight to her chest. "I have no clothes. My dress is on the floor of your car, and apparently, my panties are still out by the pool. You can't expect me to wear them before their washed."

He runs his hand through his hair and smiles back at her as he grabs his phone. "No, I don't expect you to do that.

I'll take care of your clothing." Dialling a number, he puts his phone to his ear. "Good morning Natasha. I need you to send a few outfits over to the house that will fit Rebecca, and I need you to put a rush on those." He pauses briefly, listening to what's being said on the other end. "Right. Use your best discretion. Gucci will be fine. At least three full outfits for today, two casual and be sure to include a dress. Oh, and don't forget the undergarments and a bathing suit. She'll be needing a full wardrobe, but that will do for today." He pauses briefly to listen as he walks toward his dresser. 'Yes, as soon as possible. Thank you." He hangs up his phone and smiles, tossing her one of his t-shirts. "You'll have to throw this on for now. We'll shower after breakfast. Your clothes should be here by then."

Throwing his t-shirt over her head, she pulls herself out of bed. "I have no underwear."

With a sly grin, he slides his hand between her thighs, sweeping his thumb through her folds. "Mmm. Damn, the things that I would love to do to you right now." He sucks his thumb into his mouth and winks. "Unfortunately, we have Max waiting for us downstairs at the moment, and we have a car to find." He kisses her forehead and pats her bottom. "Now, let's go before I take what's rightfully mine. I really have no qualms with Max's persistent banging on the bedroom door."

Rebecca's jaw suddenly becomes unhinged as she watches the cocky grin form across his face. Cupping her chin, he lifts her slack jaw and plants a hard kiss on her lips. "Oh, Rebecca, don't look so surprised. If I recall correctly, you didn't check off any boxes before you signed our contract last night. That means I have zero restrictions when it comes to your body for the next 30 days."

Rebecca is suddenly finding it difficult to swallow. She never even read the list, only two items. She grabs his arm and gazes up at him with pleading eyes. "Aiden, I jumped the gun on signing that contract. I never even read the list. Can't I at least go over the list and make my choices now?"

His laugh sounds almost sinister as he pulls her into his chest and brushes the hair from her face. "Oh, no, Baby. It doesn't work that way. Like I said last night, don't forget it can't be changed once it's signed. Besides, you're not a child, remember? You know how contracts work."

His cobalt eyes show just a touch of compassion as he strokes her hair. "Okay, I'll tell you what. I'm going to be generous here and go against my own policy. I'll let you look it over and check off just one definite no when we get back home."

Her brows draw together, and you'd swear she may as well have just stomped her foot. "But, Aiden, there had to be at least fifty items listed on that page!"

Taking her hand, he leads her toward the door. "Now, thanks to my generosity, you'll only have to worry about forty-nine of them," he says with a chuckle. "Let's be honest, you're not even sure of what you like or don't like yet. Now, let's go get something to eat."

Well, I'm sure there's nothing to worry about. He was such a gentleman last night. I can see him throwing a little oral into the mix. Maybe even a vibrator. Shit, I can live with that. That sounds like it might even be a lot of fun.

Max is sitting at the kitchen table with a cup of coffee when they walk in. Gesturing toward the coffee pot with his cup, he scans Rebecca from head to toe while she watches a slow sexy smile form across his handsome face. "There's coffee in the pot gorgeous."

Aiden pulls out a chair and puts his hand on her shoulder. "Sit, I'll bring the coffee over." His eyes cut to Max. "Don't you have somewhere else to be?"

"Nope. That's why I thought I'd come for breakfast and see why you needed a month off." His deep blue eyes lock with Rebecca's, and he smirks. "Now that I understand the need for a holiday, where's my breakfast, bro? I'm starving."

Setting the coffee on the table, Aiden makes it a point to ignore Max completely. "What would you like for breakfast, Rebecca? I can make you bacon and eggs, or maybe you'd like some pancakes."

Max chuckles. "Hey, Becca. Since you have all the pull with that pussy of yours, can you pick bacon and eggs, please?"

Rebecca can't help but smile. Max seems to have the ability to piss Aiden off easily.

Picking up a spoon from the table, Aiden chucks it at Max. "Shut the fuck up! Your 29 years old, not 19 anymore, Max. Have some fucking respect or leave."

Laughing, Max holds up his hands as if to surrender. It's not hard to tell this is a customary game. Trying to diffuse the sibling tension building around the table, Rebecca reaches for Aiden's hand and gives it a light kiss. "I can't believe you didn't tell me you had a twin. You two are obviously identical. Damn, I'd love just to have a sibling, but a twin. That must be amazing." She gives Max a bright smile then looks over at Aiden. "You know what? Bacon and eggs really does sound great. Why don't I give you a hand?"

As she starts to stand, Aiden rests his hand on her shoulder. "Oh, no. I'm not having Max ogle you while you make his damn breakfast. You sit and enjoy your coffee. Just let me know if he gets out of line."

I'm finding Max to be quite an interesting guy. There's no mistaking they're twins, but there are definitely some differences. Max wears his hair a bit longer, and his beard isn't as well kept as Aiden's. From what I can see, it looks as if they may have the same tattoos. However, they have entirely different personalities. Max is rough around the edges and quite boisterous. He's not refined like Aiden. I'm not even sure Max is the type to own a suit. He seems like more of the jeans and t-shirt kind of guy, the kind that openly says things like pussy without batting an eye. While Aiden is more of a gentleman. He doesn't talk like Max, and he certainly wouldn't openly ogle a woman like Max just did this morning. My summation, Max, is the hot dirty side of the Collins brothers.

Shaking Rebecca from her mental comparison, Max slips a card into the palm of her hand and looks at her matter-of-factly. "Listen, Princess. If Aiden ever mistreats you in any way, you call me. I'll gladly come to get you, no questions asked." She bursts out laughing as a roll of paper towel flies across the kitchen, hitting Max in the head.

Aiden's deep voice rumbles from the other side of the kitchen island. "Max! I said, knock it off!"

It's not hard to tell Max gets a thrill out of pissing off his brother. "So, tell me. Where did Aiden find a pretty little thing like you anyway?"

She's about to answer when Aiden appears at her side with plates and utensils. "This is the little beauty I told you about before you left for Seattle. Remember, the young lady that spilled her latte on me at the office?" He smiles at his brother, and suddenly it looks like something in Max's demeanour changes.

Leaning back in his chair, Max rubs his chin and smiles mischievously at her. "Well, shit! So, you're the infamous latte beauty."

With a hint of embarrassment, Rebecca nods. "Yeah, I guess I am."

Oh my god! How many people has he told about my ruining his suit?

Aiden places a bowl of scrambled eggs and a plate of bacon on the table and takes his seat. Taking Rebecca's hand, he kisses it lightly. "Her name is Rebecca. Use it." He waves his hand in the air as if to close the conversation. "Now, forget about the damn latte incident and eat. Rebecca and I are going out after breakfast." As Aiden reaches for his fork, the doorbell chimes. He takes a deep breath and tosses his napkin onto the table. Looking over at Max, he gives him a taunting smile and places his hand on Rebecca's shoulder. "Ahh, that must be your clothes. I'll be right back."

Rebecca takes a bite of her bacon and glances up to find Max staring. The urge to break the silence overwhelms her, and she has to speak. "So, you and Aiden are partners then? I mean, at Collins Enterprises."

Nodding, he shovels a forkful of eggs into his mouth, chews once and swallows.

Damn, this boy is a beast.

"Yeah, I guess you could say that." He sits back for a minute, studying her before he goes back to eating his breakfast. "Nah, you know what? It's Aiden's company.

Natasha will call me in if Aiden's away, which is never." He meets Rebecca's eyes. "That's one of the reasons I'm here so early this morning." Smiling, he shrugs. "Anyway, I only check with him, so I'm really not sure why she bothers."

Aiden sits back down to join them and picks up his fork. "Who do you check with?"

Max leans back and takes a sip of his coffee. "Oh, we were just talking about the company. Where are you two off to today anyway?"

"Well, I owe Rebecca a car. I accidentally had hers towed and promised to replace it."

Rebecca can feel herself stiffen as she glares over at him. "That's a lie, Aiden! It wasn't accidental at all." Suddenly she begins to think of where she'd be right now if not for him having it towed. She knows all too well she would have fallen for Alex's nonsense like she always does. She would have regrettably woken up beside him this morning.

Her face softens as Aiden takes her hand with a smirk. "Right. Well, tomato tomáto Rebecca. I still owe you a car."

She shrugs. "I actually don't mind your chauffeur services. I have nowhere to go that you won't be accompanying me, at least for the next month. So there's really no rush. Besides, I'm not even mad anymore," she says, looking at Aiden out of the corner of her eye as she takes a sip of her coffee.

Max picks up his coffee mug and holds it up to Aiden with a chuck of his chin. "Shit, bro, you must have been top of your game last night. Personally, I'd cut your sac off if you had my car towed."

Aiden smirks as he scans Rebecca's face. He knows all too well that she's referring to the terms of the contract, but his mind is stuck on last night. He can already picture a future with her. "Yeah, well, I'm not playing a game, Bro."

Rebecca clears her throat as she takes a drink of her coffee. She doesn't want this conversation to get too deep, especially with Max as a participant. "Okay then, what kind of car are we getting? The same type as the one I had?"

Smiling, Aiden looks up at her from under his brow. "I'm afraid they don't make cars like that anymore, Rebecca."

"Are you going to Three Points downtown? I heard they have the new E400 convertibles in stock. She'd look hot behind the wheel of one of those," Max says, giving her a wink. "Trust me. You want this car." Rebecca opens her mouth as if she's about to say something when Max raises his hands defensively. "I'm just trying to help you out here, babe. Think big. He can afford it."

Did he just call me 'babe'?

"Well, I'm sure we'll be able to get something close to what I had." She stands and lays her hand on Aiden's shoulder. "I'm going to go for a quick shower and get ready now that my clothes are here." Her eyes shift to Max, and she gives him a bright smile. "Great to meet you, Max."

Hoping Max will have left by the time she gets back downstairs, she heads up to Aiden's room. The ensuite is enormous. There is a thick glass brick divider that separates the toilet from the bathing area. Past the glass wall is a double soaker tub and shower with a cascading water wall between the two. It's a dream bathroom, to say the least. Turning on the water, she strips off Aiden's t-shirt and climbs into the massive glass stall. As she's lathering her hair, she hears the bathroom door click, accompanied by Aiden's deep voice. His fingers dance across her ribs, making her squirm and giggle. "Hey, how come you didn't wait for me?"

"I'm sorry. I knew you wanted to go, and you had your brother here." She finishes rinsing her hair and turns to face him. "I would have waited if I knew you wanted me to."

He takes the soap from the dish, rolling it in his hand to build a good lather. "Max is going to come with us to the dealership." Returning the soap, he reaches down and taps her inner thigh. "Spread your legs. Max really knows his cars, and I think he could be an asset in finding the right vehicle for you. Go ahead and rinse," he says, running his hand under the water.

She lifts her leg, resting her foot on the ledge to rinse as Aiden steps forward to stand between her thighs. His once flaccid member is now firm and pointing toward its desire. He gently holds her jaw in his hand and licks a droplet of water from her top lip. Slowly releasing her chin as a shiver slides down her spine. The back of his hand glides over her breast, pausing briefly to caress her nipple, and coaxing out a moan. She's about to lower her leg when Aiden stops her. "Don't move. Stay exactly like that."

Nervous anticipation fills her stomach as she watches him kneel in front of her. "Here?"

When the warmth of his tongue slides between her folds, she grasps the handrail on the shower door to steady herself and closes her eyes. "Holy — shit."

He slips his finger into her opening, slowly gliding it in and out while his tongue magically twists around her swollen bud. She can feel the waves of excitement begin to radiate from her core as her body starts to hum with energy. Her legs begin to tremble, and her hand falls to the top of his head. She grabs a fist full of his hair and tries pushing him back, but he's not about to let her pull away. Aiden grabs her by the ass and pulls her closer, burying his face deep between her thighs as she cries out in a broken airy gasp. "Oh — My — God. Yes!"

Rebecca's body is still pulsating when Aiden stands and licks his lips with a grin. "I don't think you need to worry about that item anymore." He teases her nipple between his thumb and forefinger, using his other hand to settle himself against her entrance. "See, it's all about discovery."

She's still trying to catch her breath when her heavy-lidded eyes focus on him. "Aiden…" But before she can finish what she's about to say, his mouth covers hers, swallowing her words with a searing kiss. He places one hand on her lower back, and the other in her hair, thrusting into her. Once again, she's robbed of all rational thought.

"Jesus, Rebecca. You feel so fucking good." His hands slide down her back to cradle her bottom as he grinds himself into her. "Wrap your legs around me, baby."

Her arms instinctively wrap around his shoulders, and her legs anchor around his waist. "Oh my god, Aiden — don't stop!" Shockwaves rip through her, and her muscles tense. As her feral moans echo through the bathroom, he knows that at this very moment, he owns her body. Her head falls back, and she fights to keep hold of him.

He drives forward, and she feels the coolness of the tiles hit her back each time he grinds himself deeper. "That's it, Baby. If you could only see just how fucking hot you look right now."

Breathing in, he takes in the vision he has before him. Rebecca's flesh is flushed from the heat of the shower and her recent release. Her head is tilted, resting against the wall. She has her eyes closed, and her lips are slightly parted. The wet strands of her long blond hair hug her breasts as they bounce with every movement.

Keeping his eyes on her, his thrusts become harder and more determined. A final push forward, and he holds her tight against him as he explodes. Her vaginal walls scream with a painful pleasure she will now always crave as her muscles begin to spasm around him uncontrollably.

"Fuck, Rebecca. You could become my addiction," he pants out breathlessly before his head drops to the crevice of her neck.

God, I hope so because you're quickly becoming mine.

Once the orgasmic haze clears, embarrassment starts to set in. "Oh, shit! You said your brother is still here waiting for us."

He shrugs, wrapping a towel around his waist. An impressive impression of his semi-hard manhood stares back at Rebecca as he turns to face her. "Well, I hate to break it to you, baby, but I'm pretty sure he didn't think I was just coming up to wash your back." Fixing his gaze on her as she slides on the pair of white short-shorts Natasha had sent over, his eyes light up. "Wow. Turn around and let me see those."

Narrowing her eyes at him, she twists her head over her shoulder to have a look in the mirror at her bottom. She usually wears her shorts a bit longer, but they don't seem too extreme. Turning toward him like he's asked, she wiggles her bottom with a giggle before turning back to face him. "What's the problem? Do they meet your approval?" she asks, pulling on the tank top that Natasha sent with them.

Aiden rubs the palm of his hand across his forehead. "God damn it! I'm gonna have to kill Max before the day is over. I can just feel it." He almost looks pained, knowing his brother will be checking her out.

Laughing, Rebecca grabs his hand from his forehead. "Oh, come on. Max just loves to get you going. Anyone can see that."

Aiden nods, cupping her face with his hands as he kisses her. "Mm-hmm. Let's go get this over with so we can lose him." Taking her by the hand, he leads her downstairs.

They find Max waiting in the living room watching TV. He turns around with a huge shit-eating grin. "I had to turn on the TV to try and drown out all the moaning. You should really think about investing in soundproofing, Aiden." Heat instantly rushes to Rebecca's cheeks. She tries to divert her gaze, but it's too late. Max's eyes meet hers, and he winks with a sly smile. "You good now, princess?"

Shit! God, please strike me dead right now!

Rebecca slowly slides behind Aiden's big frame to hide from Max's scrutinizing eye.

Aiden tucks her into his side with a slight chuckle. "Jesus, Max. Shut up. You're embarrassing her."

Max puts his hands up in surrender. "Becca, I'm sorry. I just joke around a lot. Do you forgive me?"

He extends his hand to her with an exaggerated pout. As she accepts his hand, he smiles. "But seriously, that was the hottest fucking orgasm I've heard out of a woman to date! I'm gonna be walking around with a chub all day, just thinking about it."

Okay. Its official, I have never been so embarrassed in my life.

Aiden swats him in the back of the head. "Jesus, Max! Fucking knock it off!" Shaking his head, he pulls her back from Max. "Just ignore him. He obviously needs to get laid."

Max grunts heading for the door. "Absolutely, I'm obviously in need now. If you ask me, Aiden has his priorities in his ass, princess. I'd just order you a car offline and let you drive me all fucking day." He grabs his groin and smiles with a snap of his head. "Mmm!"

Bounding forward, Aiden moves so fast, swiping Max's legs out from under him that Max has no time to react.

He lands with a loud thud on the floor, looking a little stunned. "What-the-fuck, Aiden?!"

"I said, shut the fuck up, Max!"

He takes Rebecca's hand, leading her toward the door. As they pass Max, Aiden glances at him with a sideways grin. "You coming or what?"

All her embarrassment gone, Rebecca can't help but laugh. These two are classic comedic brother material. Max gains his feet and straightens himself. "Of course. How else can I watch that sweet ass all day?"

Aiden stops and shoots him a warning glance. Max stops dead in his tracks, throwing his hands up in defence. "Okay, I'm done, I'm done."

Chapter 5 – The Car

When they arrive at the dealership, Max jumps out of his Hummer and walks up to Rebecca. He throws his arm around her shoulder and reminds her. "Now, don't forget what I said. You want to see the E400, and you want that baby fully loaded." He chucks his chin at Aiden. "Let the lady ask for the car."

Rebecca eyes the brothers for confidence as the salesman approaches. Aiden gives her a reassuring smile, while Max mouths 'E400' waving her forward with a nod. Straightening her shoulders, she greets the salesman and asks to see the new Mercedes E400. Max quickly chimes in behind her, "Make sure that baby is fully loaded. If the lady likes it, we'll be taking it with us today."

The salesman looks Rebecca up and down with an appreciative eye and grins slyly. With a nod, he looks past her at Aiden and Max, then stutters slightly. "Y-Yes ma'am. Would you like to test drive the convertible model or the hardtop?" he asks, allowing his sly grin to return.

Max steps up beside her and addresses the salesman. "I'm not sure we caught your name. Did you give it?"

"I introduced myself to the lady, Sir. My name is Lance."

"Okay, Lance," Max sneers. "She'll definitely want the convertible model. Oh, and we'll be coming along for the test drive. So make sure it's a 4-seater and wipe that fucking grin off your face."

The salesman gives him a nervous nod and turns to leave. "Of course, Sir. I'll be right back."

Aiden laughs, tucking Rebecca into his side. "Jesus, Max. You're gonna make the poor guy piss his pants."

Leaning against one of the new vehicles parked along the rim of the lot, Max folds his arms. "Whatever. That guy is a weasel. He was nothing short of licking his lips when he eyed Becca. Let him fucking squirm."

Smiling, Aiden checks Rebecca out with his own appreciative eye. "She's hot. Of course, he's gonna check her out. As long as he doesn't try to touch her." He points his finger at Max, drawing his brows together. "That goes for you too. We're not kids anymore. She's with me."

Max pushes himself off the car he's been leaning on and smirks. "Come on, Aiden, we're brothers. Nan and Pop always taught us that sharing is caring."

Clearing her throat, Rebecca puts her hands in the air to make her presence known. "Uh, guys! I'm right here. Do you mind?"

The sound of gravel crunching under tires alerts them to the salesman driving up in a sleek red convertible. Rebecca nearly jumps out of her skin. It's freaking gorgeous! It doesn't even begin to compare to her old Mazda in the slightest. "Holy shit!

You're not seriously considering buying this car, are you Aiden?" she asks, clinging to his arm as they approach the vehicle.

He opens the driver's door and motions for her to get in. "That all depends on if you like the way it handles or not. You obviously like the look of it." He slides into the passenger seat, shoving the salesman into the back with Max. "Let's go find out."

She pulls out of the driveway and onto Government St., one of the busier streets in Victoria. With the amount of traffic, there's no way she can get a good feel of how the car will handle on a typical drive. Aiden gestures for her to take it onto the highway, and she doesn't skip a beat. Rebecca's dying to open it up. Turning onto the on-ramp, she gives it some gas.

It's smooth,

It's sleek,

It's fast, and she loves it!

She glances over at Aiden with a wide smile, and that's all it takes. The look on his face says it all –

It's Sold!

Pulling off at the next exit, she turns around and heads back to the dealership. As they're exiting the car, Aiden looks over at Rebecca with a smile. "Well, Lance. It's your lucky day. It seems the lady loves the car. Why don't you get the paperwork ready so we can take it with us?"

Rebecca can't hide her excitement. She leaps into his arms. "Oh my god! I love it! I never expected something so extravagant, but I absolutely love it! Thank you!"

Aiden can't help but laugh as she kisses him wildly. "I'm glad you like it, but it's just a car, Rebecca."

"Like it? I love it!"

Max holds his arms out to her. "Hey, what about me? I told you about the damn car. Don't I deserve some lovin'?"

Aiden folds his arms. "You better watch it. If you piss her off, she has a killer right hook." Rebecca pats Aiden on the chest and walks over to Max. "He's right, he deserves a thank you."

She walks over to him with her arms outstretched. "Well, come on down here, you big lug."

Max leans down, giving Aiden a shit-eating grin, and Rebecca wraps her arms around his neck, placing a chaste kiss on his cheek. "Thanks, Max. I wouldn't have known what car to ask for. It's perfect!" She lets go of his neck and starts to turn away when he scoops her up into his arms whirling her around in a tight hug.

"See that, Aiden! I got a hug and a kiss." He plants a hard kiss on her cheek. "Princess, I've decided we've gotta keep ya. Our family could use a sweet female around." Setting her down on her feet, he pats her bottom and kisses his teeth with an approving nod. "This one is definitely a keeper, bro. I'm giving you a fair warning. If you set her loose, I'm chasing after her."

Rebecca can't help but laugh. "Thanks for your approval Max," she says, walking back into Aiden's arms.

She really does love the banter between these two brothers. Their camaraderie is incredible. From what she's seen so far, she'd love to be part of their family if given a real chance. Unfortunately, she'll only be a part of their family for the next month. Unless Aiden decides he wants to keep her, but what are the odds of that?

It takes Lance, the salesman, about an hour to complete the paperwork and clear Aiden's cheque. Once it's finally done, he hands Rebecca the ownership and keys to her brand new metallic red convertible. Aiden may have written the cheque, but the ownership is in her name, and it's paid in full.

Oh my god! It's really mine!

As Rebecca sinks into her new car, Aiden leans on her driver's door. "Why don't we stop for lunch?" He tugs on the strap of her tank top. "Obviously, we'll be looking for someplace that offers casual dining."

"We can stop at the Purple Lion. Emma's working, and I'd love to show her my new car," she says with a bright smile.

Max taps her passenger door. "Do they serve food and beer?"

"Mm-hmm." She nods.

"That's good enough for me!" Hopping into the passenger seat of her car, Max slaps the dash. "Well, what are we waiting for? Let's go. If Emma is anything like you, I'll have her for lunch since all of a sudden, Aiden forgot how to share." He waggles his brows with a sly smile.

Aiden shoots him a dirty look. His voice anything but calm. "Get the fuck out of her car. You can drive your damn self."

Max sympathetically tilts his head at Aiden. "Aw, are you afraid I'll steal your lady, bro?' Cause with that attitude, you should be."

Storming over to the passenger side, Aiden opens the door and grabs him by the arm. "Alright, Max. That's enough. Get out of the fucking car."

Laughing as he steps out, blowing her a kiss on his way back to his Hummer. "Okay, I guess I'll meet you there, princess."

She shakes her head, looking up at Aiden. "Are you going to follow me, or am I going to follow you?"

He kisses her softly on the cheek and turns to head back to his car. "You lead the way."

Watching in her rear-view mirror, she catches a glimpse of Aiden and Max playing musical lanes behind her.

Damn, these two can be so childish.

I love it!

Sigh —

They pull into the parking lot at the Purple Lion, and Max parks so tight against the driver's door of Aiden's car that he has no choice but to climb out the passenger side. As Aiden struggles to pull his big body across the center console trying to get to the passenger door, Max and Rebecca stand chuckling. They watch him periodically shake his fist at Max and yell out threats until he finally kicks open the passenger door. "I'm only going to put up with so much, Max. For this little stunt, lunch is on you. I'll have one of everything on the fucking menu!"

"Yeah yeah! You could have chosen another spot. Anyway, let's go, you pissed around so much it's almost supper time for Christ sakes." Crossing his feet at his ankles, Max folds his arms calmly across his chest. "Seriously, princess. How do you put up with his whining?"

Walking over to Aiden, she slings her arm through his. "You two are bloody hilarious. I can't imagine what you must have put your poor parents through."

"You mean our poor Grandparents. Our parents died when we were eight. Aiden didn't tell you?" Max says, throwing his arm over her shoulder as they walk into the bar.

Aiden lifts Max's arm from her shoulder and replaces it with his own. "No. It's not really something that has ever come up."

Great! Foot meet mouth.

"God. I'm sorry, guys," she says as a feeling of guilt smacks her in the face.

Max shrugs. "Don't be. It was for the best. Besides, they aren't technically dead. They're just dead to us." He smiles and claps his hands. "Anyway, that's enough of that dreary shit. I need food and beer! That's why we're here, right?"

Rebecca spots Emma darting toward them with an anxious look on her face. "Hey, Becca. I don't finish until later, and I don't think you'll want to eat here right now. Alex and the band are here. You might want to take Aiden somewhere else to eat. I can't have you guys fighting here. I need my job."

"Relax, Em. We have no intention of fighting with Alex." Rebecca turns back to gain confirmation from Aiden and Max. "Right, guys?" Both brothers stand with their arms folded and nod. "See. We just came to have some lunch and show you my new car." She grabs hold of Emma's arm, turning toward Max and Aiden. "Anyway, this is Max. Aiden's twin brother. Max, this is my best friend and roommate, Emma." Max nods to be polite, but there is something about the way she lifted herself off that guy by the back of the bar and sprinted toward Becca that didn't sit well with him. In fact, there is something about her that he simply doesn't like. Rebecca's voice breaks through his thoughts. "Why don't you two go grab us a table while I show Em my car?"

Aiden smiles and kisses her on the forehead. "That sounds good, baby. Don't be long."

Max's gaze is still anchored on Emma when Aiden tugs him toward an empty table. "Jesus, bro. What's with you?"

When Rebecca and Emma get out to the parking lot, Emma's jaw hits the ground. "Holy sheep shit, Becca!

Aiden bought you this?"

Dancing around the car, as if she were a teenager, Rebecca's face lights up. "I know, right! Isn't it amazing, Em! I fucking love it!"

"Yeah, that's a pretty sweet ride. What did you have to do for it, Becca?" Alex's voice resonates from behind her like a foghorn.

"Alex! Stop!" Emma slams into him, shoving him back toward the building. "Just go back inside, Alex!"

He pushes Emma aside, continuing toward Rebecca until they're standing toe-to-toe. His angry eyes are staring deep into hers. He's so close she can feel his breath as he speaks. "Emma, I said, go inside. Becca and I need to talk."

Rebecca watches Emma run inside, and she's pretty sure it won't be too long before Aiden and Max appear. She takes a step back, trying to manoeuvre around him, but he steps back with her. Backing her against the car, he cages her in with his arms. "Why don't you take me for a drive? You know, show me how this baby handles." His voice sounds different, not that kind, sweet tone that she's used to. Today it's low and has an untrusting undertone.

Thankfully, out of the corner of her eye, Rebecca sees the bar doors swing open. Two big bodies are strutting their way, and they don't look happy. In fact, they look rather pissed. She hears Aiden's deep voice call out to her. "Are you okay, Baby?"

Before she can say anything, Alex spits back. "She's fine, Daddy Warbucks. We're just fucking talking."

Aiden closes in quickly and stands beside Rebecca. "I wasn't talking to you, now was I, rockstar?"

Max grabs Alex by the scruff of the neck, pulling him away from Rebecca as Aiden reaches for her hand, holding her tight to his chest. He brushes the hair from her cheek and kisses her forehead. "Are you okay? Did he touch you?"

A loud bang echoes and she jumps, not realizing right away it's the impact of Alex's head against the hood of Aiden's car. "Stay away from Becca. She doesn't want to talk to you anymore. Understand?" Max growls.

"Fuck off, you bohemian!" Alex spits back, trying to kick out of Max's grip. "She's mine. We just had a disagreement. We need to sort some things out. Tell them, Becca."

Mine?!

That gets her blood flowing again. Rebecca twists out of Aiden's arms and stands in front of Alex with her nostrils flaring. "Yours?! I'm not yours, Alex! We haven't been dating in over a year. We agreed to stay in touch with each other when you left, but that never happened. In fact, I haven't spoken to you or so much as seen you in a year. Anytime I have seen you, you've always had some tramp draped over you. I have no interest in you or your lifestyle. I'm with Aiden now. So get fucking used to it!"

Who the hell does he think he is?!

Max slams Alex against Aiden's car one more time. "Did you hear the lady that time?"

"Yeah, I fucking heard her!"

Max lets him go, and Alex stares at Rebecca, the anger now removed and in its place stands something resembling hurt. "Real nice, Becca. I thought we were supposed to get married." He starts walking toward the bar. "What about that? Huh?" He yells, glancing back. Resting his hand on the door handle, he turns back to face her and hollers, "Hey, Becca. Just tell me one thing. Are you at least thinking of me when he's fucking you?"

Rebecca gasps, folding herself into Aiden's chest.

"Wow, now that was a dramatic exit," Max says, folding his arms across his chest as he watches him disappear into the bar.

Aiden's arms wrap around her. "Don't let him get to you, baby." He gives her a kiss on the cheek. "Let's just go eat. We have a table full of food in there, and I'm pretty sure he's not going to bother us anymore."

Max strolls up beside them and pats her on the back. "Yeah, this stupid fucker really ordered one of everything on the god damn menu. So I hope you're hungry."

When they get back inside, Rebecca notices their one table has now turned into three with all the plates of food Aiden has ordered. She turns to look at him and lets out a small laugh. "I can't believe you really ordered one of everything."

"Oh, please. Max had it coming," he says, looking over at her with a grin. Rebecca takes a quick glance around the restaurant, thankful to see that there is no sign of Alex. Pulling out her chair, Aiden grabs her attention. "Have a seat, baby. Here comes your friend with the rest of our lunch."

Emma saunters over and drops another plate on their already full tables with a pathetic attempt at a sympathetic smile. She puts her arms around Rebecca and gives her a tight squeeze. "I'm so sorry, Becca. I tried to warn you. He hasn't been himself all morning."

Rebecca lets her off way too easy for Max's liking when she says, "It's fine. It's not your fault, Em."

Max grabs Emma's arm before she can walk away and glares up at her. "Actually, Emma. Don't you think as

Becca's so-called best friend, you should tell her the real reason you tried to get her to leave when we came in?"

Becca gives Max a bewildered look while Emma tries to pull out of his grasp, shaking her head. "I don't know what you're talking about."

Her voice just went up an octave. She knows exactly what I'm fucking talking about.

"Oh, no?" Becca glances between Max and Emma, a bit bewildered. "Now that I know who Alex is. Weren't you the one that unlocked your tongue from his and scurried over to us when we walked in here?" Her face instantly turns a deep crimson, and she's unable to meet Rebecca's eyes.

She drops her head in her hands. "Becca. I... He was upset. God. I'm so sorry."

Rebecca lifts her chin and forces a smile. "I don't care about Alex. He's not mine. We haven't been together for a long time." She raises her hand toward Emma with a look of disgust. "But, I have to admit. I would have never thought you would go for my leftovers. Especially when you knew the way he treated me. I think you two deserve each other."

She throws her hand up, stopping Emma from saying anything further. "Don't! Just keep him out of my room until I can move my stuff out of the house."

There is nothing else Emma can say. Dropping her eyes to

the floor, she keeps her head low as she turns and walks back toward the kitchen.

I knew there was something about her I didn't like.

Max gives Becca a sympathetic look. "I'm really sorry, Princess. I just couldn't allow them both to dog you like that." Rebecca rewards him with a small smile and a nod, and for Max, that's enough. For now.

They finish what they can of the food surrounding them, leaving a ton of food behind and head back to Rebecca's place to grab some of her clothes. She leads them up to her bedroom, and Max immediately flops down on her bed with his hands clasped behind his head. Aiden leans up against the doorframe impatiently with his arms folded and watches her as she moves about the room. She's been back and forth from the bathroom to the closet and the dresser, packing things up for about 20 minutes when Aiden finally rolls his head, letting it rest against the frame. "Come on, baby. Just grab a couple outfits and maybe a spare bathing suit. I told you, Natasha has already ordered you a complete wardrobe. It should be delivered to the house by tomorrow."

She turns to face him and places her hand on her hip. "Aiden, I have clothes. I don't need a whole new wardrobe."

Max props himself up on his elbows and shakes his head. "Becca, Becca, Becca. Let him buy the damn clothes." Scanning the length of her body, he meets her eyes. "If Natasha picked out what you're wearing now." He clicks his tongue with a shake of his head and a wink. "Please. Let him buy the damn clothes."

Aiden shoots him a dirty look. "I think it's time for you to go home, Maxwell."

Max lets out a hearty laugh as he lifts himself from the bed. "Yeah, you're right. It actually is time for me to head out. I've got some shit to do." He gives Rebecca another wink. "See you later, princess." He whacks Aiden on the back on his way out. "Latez, bro."

Chapter 6 – The Dirty Girl Scout

Shortly after Max heads home, Aiden and Rebecca drive back to his place. When she walks in, she flops down on the sofa and watches as Aiden opens his desk drawer. Turning back to face her, he hands her a copy of the contract. "Here, I believe I owe you an item."

He struts over to the bar and pours two glasses of wine. Handing one to her, he takes a seat in the chair across from where she's sitting. "Be sure to choose wisely, baby. You only get one."

Rebecca glances down at the page in front of her and spots one word that immediately sends chills up her spine.

'Anal'

Is he fucking serious?

Looking at him from under her brows, she feels the heat creep across her cheeks. "Aiden…"

A sly smile spreads across his lips as he raises his glass to his mouth to take a generous drink. "Rebecca, you only get one." He slowly articulates. "I have never allowed anyone to renegotiate a contract once it's been signed." Setting his glass down on the table beside him, he clasps his hands on the arms of his chair. His intense gaze never leaving hers. "I guess you can always leave it completely open. I have no issues with being able to explore freely. After all, I'm not a brute. I'm sure you must know by now that my intention is not to hurt you."

I do believe he has no intention of hurting me, but I'm still not sure about anal.

"Aiden, there's a whole section dedicated to Anal alone!" She stares at him, her eyes almost pleading. "If I check off the anal heading, does that cancel all of the items listed under that section?"

I know I sound like I'm whining, I am, and I don't care.

A smirk graces his face as he walks over to sit beside her on the sofa. "Is that honestly your biggest fear?" he asks, taking the paper from her hands and holding it up to examine it.

She shrugs. "I'm not sure. I still haven't read the whole damn thing. I just know that the thought of anal scares the hell out of me."

The craziest part is, it kind of excites me too. I can feel that annoying little pulse between my thighs when I think of it. In fact, I am almost certain if I were to check my panties, they would probably be damp. But that's definitely not something I'm going to tell him. I can explore that when I'm ready, not at his whim.

Aiden tosses the paper to the floor like it's trash. "This thing is useless anyway if you really think about it."

Her eyes grow wide as they follow the page to the floor. She's about ready to freak out when she decides to sit back and wait for his explanation instead. She stares at him doubtingly, yet curious to see where he's going with this. He brushes the hair back from her cheek. "Look, let's be honest. You don't even know your limits. Why don't we forget about that page, and we can learn your limits together?"

A slight feeling of relief washes over her, and a smile instantly stretches across her face as she nods. "Okay. I think I can live with that."

Then suddenly, that word flashes before her eyes again.

'Anal'

"Wait, but..."

He places his finger over her lips to stop her. "Shh."

Kissing her lightly, he stands and walks toward the bar, then pauses and raises his brow at her. "We can gently explore all your limits, Rebecca."

Refilling his glass, Aiden looks over at her as a slight smirk forms on his lips. "Even though you have my word that I would never put you in danger or harm you in any way. You should know that I will test your limits from time to time.

Come on, Becca, swallow. You were born with the ability. It's a natural god damn reflex. You can do it.

Emptying her wine glass in one swallow. She holds it up to Aiden for a refill. He lifts his brow, glancing at her out of the corner of his eye with a soft chuckle. "Are you thirsty?"

Trying her best to ignore the implications of his previous statement, she clears her throat and forces a smile. "Mm-hmm. Maybe a little."

Aiden waves her over to where he's standing behind the bar. "Come join me. I make the absolute best ice cream floats. I'm gonna teach you my secrets. You'll never think of ice cream floats the same again. I promise."

As Rebecca walks up beside him, he grabs her by the waist and lifts her onto the bar making her squeal. "Jesus, Aiden!"

His warm breath feathers across her neck as he leans into her. "It's okay, baby. I've got you. Just lean back and hold that rail behind you." Running his hands over her hips to her inner thighs, he slowly spreads her legs and stands between them. His lust-filled eyes scan her body as he grins with approval. "There. Now stay just like that." He reaches under the bar pulling out a pair of scissors, and Rebecca's heart begins to race.

She quickly sits up, closing her legs against his waist. "What the fuck, Aiden?!"

His face tightens, and he rests his hand on her chest to hold her in place. "Rebecca, I already assured you I would never hurt you. I'm a man of my word, but I will tie you in place if you're not going to do as I ask." Cupping her chin, he gives her a reassuring kiss. "Now, go back to your position."

Unsure how this man can have such an effect on her, she does her best to try and ignore the persistent twitch between her thighs.

Focusing on repositioning herself, she leans back. Grabbing the rail and opens her legs to return to the position she was in before he startled her. "But I thought we were making ice cream floats."

Aiden smiles, running the scissors along the outside of her shorts. "Don't worry, baby. We will. I need to prepare a couple of things first." She watches him carefully as he slips his finger under the waistband of her shorts and slides it to one side, holding the material out from her body. The feel of cold metal from the scissors slides along her outer thigh as he slices through the side of her shorts.

"What the hell, Aiden?! These are new!"

Two more snips, and he slices through the waistband, completely opening the one side of her new shorts.

"Relax. I'll buy you more. Besides, Max likes these way too much."

He repeats the process on the opposite side, flapping the front panel of her shorts forward. Lifting the elastic of her panties off her hips, he snips each side and lets them fall between her thighs with a satisfied smile. Rebecca's heart begins to race as his eyes meet hers. Her eyes drop to the scissors, following his every move as he brings them up to the center of her tank top, she gasps. "Honestly, Rebecca. You need to learn to trust me."

With a couple of snips, he severs her tank top and bra. Between the sudden exposure and her arousal, her nipples harden so quickly they sting. He slices through the straps on her shoulders, letting it fall to the bar and leans back. "Mmm. There, now that's better."

Placing the scissors down on the bar beside her, he runs his finger through her folds, feeling her wetness. Rebecca's body ignites under his touch. His smile instantly broadens. "See, we're constantly making discoveries about what you like."

With bated breath, she watches as he lifts his finger to his lips and sucks it into his mouth with a moan. "There is truly nothing better than the taste of a woman's arousal."

Aiden has her in such a daze at this point she's unsure of how to respond. He steps back and smiles. "Right. We're making ice cream floats."

He grabs a tub of chocolate ice cream from the bar freezer and places it between her thighs with a spoon. Grabbing two large beer mugs, he sets them down beside her.

"Now, pay close attention. I think you're really going to like this."

She can't help but think of how adorable he looks as she watches him scoop ice cream into the two mugs, counting them out alternating as he goes. "One for you...One for me...Two for you...Two for me..." He glances up at her with a sly grin then scoops ice cream onto the top of her bare mound. She shrieks and tries to wiggle, but he holds her steady. "Easy now, that one is for us."

Her face tenses. "Jesus, Aiden! That's cold!"

"Of course it's cold, it's ice cream, baby. Now stay still until I'm finished." He reaches for a bottle of Amaretto and pours a shot in each mug and the smaller glass. Opening a bottle of root beer, he adds some to each cup then focuses his eyes on hers. "How are you doing? Is it still cold?"

Feeling it leak between her folds and onto the bar below, she shrugs. "Not really. It's mostly melted now, but it's making a mess."

"Mmm, yes, it is messy. I'm going to call this the Dirty Girl Scout." Rebecca scrunches up her face, and Aiden chuckles. "Don't worry. I'm going to clean you up." Holding the small glass just above her mound, he kneels and places his mouth against her bottom. Rebecca starts to pull herself up when he begins to pour the contents slowly over her, using his tongue to lap up the liquid as it runs between her folds.

"Ohh," she moans out, lying back against the rail. Emptying the glass, he sets it down on the bar. At this point, he has her wound so tight she's just about ready to hand him one of the mugs to ensure he doesn't stop, but there's no need. His head disappears, and his finger slides inside her as he completely clears any evidence of any ice cream float from between her thighs. A kaleidoscope of butterflies take flight in her stomach as that beautiful burst of nervous excitement shakes her entire body.

Holding her hips firmly, he probes deep into her opening with his magical tongue, slowly coaxing out every last wave of her orgasm. When she opens her eyes, he's hovering above her. "Mmm, best damn ice cream float I've ever tasted." Wiping the back of his hand across his chin, the corner of his mouth lifts slightly. "So, what do you think? Will you still envision a glass of pop with some ice cream when someone mentions an ice cream float?"

Looking at his glistening face, she smiles. "Well, first of all, your method of delivery is supreme, and there is absolutely no way I could think of anything but this night when someone mentions an ice cream float now." Sitting up, she reaches for one of the mugs and takes a drink. "Wow, and this actually tastes quite good. I'm impressed, baby."

Aiden's face softens as he runs his finger down her cheek. "Me too. You just called me baby."

"I'm sorry. Should I not have done that?" She searches his face looking for any signs of disdain, but instead, he seems quite pleased.

"Don't be sorry. It's fine. You just haven't called me anything other than Aiden until now." Peeling off his t-shirt, he turns his back to her and taps his shoulder. "Come on, hop up."

Looking down at her nakedness, she peers back up at him and shakes her head shyly. "I'm naked and sticky."

His head flies around, and his lip curls as he rolls his eyes. "This is not the time to be a prude. I've been inside that body. Besides, you love being naked, remember?"

With a giggle, she wraps herself around him, absorbing his warmth. "You have such a way with words, Mr. Collins." Kissing his neck, she snuggles her cheek against his warm back. "Where are you taking me?"

He strides out through the patio doors. "I'm going to take you to the hot tub to warm you up."

Standing next to the tub, he crouches to let her down and flicks the switch. She loves watching the hot tub come to life with the coloured lights dancing beneath the water. Aiden undoes his jeans and strips off his boxers then pushes the button to activate the jets. "Go on, get in. I'll grab our drinks."

Climbing in, Rebecca can't peel her eyes from Aiden's glorious body. He's a tanned, muscular perfection wrapped up in a 6'4" frame. The tattoos that grace his back dance with each movement. To put it plainly, he is the perfect dark prince from every little girl's childhood fairy-tale, and he's all hers — at least for the next month.

God, help me! I am in way too deep.

Aiden struts back to the hot tub carrying two glasses and a bottle of Whiskey. Stepping in, he gives her a sweet smile. "I thought we'd have a couple of whiskey shots tonight." Pouring them each a shot, he seals the bottle back up and drops it into the steaming tub. Handing her a glass, he holds his up to toast. "To trying new things and keeping an open mind."

Rebecca can't help but chuckle, considering their new version of ice cream floats. "How about just to us?" she asks.

Aiden nods his head side to side, clanking his glass to hers. "Yes, of course. To us."

Tipping back the glass of liquid hell, she can feel it burn the entire way down to her stomach. "Holy shit! That burns!"

He laughs, fishing out the bottle to refill their glasses

with another shot. Pouring them each a drink, he raises his glass once again to clink it with hers. His face takes on a more serious look. "Now, this... this is to discovering us."

Inviting the liquid fire into her body once again, she waits for it to hit bottom and blows out a big breath as it does. Aiden relieves her of her glass, setting it on the ledge of the tub. "Oh, yes. That stuff will definitely warm you from the inside out, but I have something that might a little more inviting that guarantees to warm you from the inside out as well. Come here." He pulls her onto his lap and presses his lips to hers. His kiss is filled with a promise of incredible passion as he positions himself beneath her. She slowly lowers herself onto him little by little, rising just enough to relieve the pressure before sinking back down until she's finally resting firmly against his groin.

He's so big

So hard

The way he grabs her hips and grinds himself into her while his tongue possesses her mouth -- it takes over her mind completely. At this moment, this is the side of Aiden Collins she can't get enough of.

Her stomach swirls with excitement, and her muscles tighten in protest as his pace begins to quicken. His breathing starts to increase as his fingers dig into her bottom, dragging her down with every upward thrust. She swears it feels like he's gained inches on his girth.

She grips his shoulders as her legs start to tremble and lets out a moan. He pushes himself deep inside her, and she can feel the tension of her imminent orgasm begin to build. Like looking down the first hill of a rollercoaster, her stomach seizes with anticipation. He lifts her slightly, driving into her with a roar, and she can feel the rush of heat flood her body. Releasing a breath she was unaware she had been holding, she gasps. "Oh – My –God Yes!"

Aiden expels a long, intense moan from somewhere deep inside as he wraps his arms around her, pulling her tight against his chest. It is the absolute hottest thing she has ever heard. It's one that can only be defined as 100% pure satisfaction. "Fuck, Baby. You are surely going to be my demise."

She runs her fingers through his damp hair and gives him a kiss. "Mmm. I hope not. You're kind of growing on this dirty Girl Scout." Lifting herself free from his lap and the hot tub, he watches her every move intently. "Hey, Aiden. Since it's still early, do you think maybe we can go for a walk?"

He steps out of the hot tub, grabbing the offered towel from her hands. "Sure, it's a nice night. We can go for a walk along the Sidney pier if you'd like. Maybe we can even make the aquarium and catch the octopus show before it closes." Smacking her bottom, he sends mixed signals through to her core. It's a wonderful cross somewhere between pleasure and pain. A sly smile spreads across his face. "The other outfit Natasha sent over this morning is on the nightstand beside the bed. Go get dressed, and we'll go."

Wanting to make the aquarium before it closes, Rebecca hurries upstairs. She slips the cute peach coloured sundress Natasha picked out for her over her head then heads for the bathroom. Remembering Aiden prefers her hair down, Rebecca leaves it loose across her shoulders and gives her makeup a quick touch up. As she takes a minute to examine her overall look in the mirror, she catches a glimpse of him stalking up behind her. Before she can turn around to face him, his arms slink around her waist. "You look beautiful. Let's go, or we'll miss the aquarium."

He's wearing a pair of slim-fitting black dress pants and a white polo shirt that shows off all his manly assets. His hair looks like he just ran his fingers through it instead of a comb, giving him that sexy 'I don't give a fuck' look. And, oh my god - the way he smells. That intoxicating spicy citrus, he's almost edible. She wraps her arms around his waist and kisses his cheek. "Mmm, I could smell you all day."

Taking her hand, he leads her out of the bathroom. "Somehow, I doubt it would stop at a smell. Let's go before we don't make it out of the house, my insatiable little monster."

She steps back, holding her hand to her chest with a stunned look on her face. "Are you complaining? Because I'm pretty sure you've created this monster stirring within, and it didn't sound or feel like your body was complaining a few minutes ago."

He stops abruptly, pulling her into his arms with a chuckle. "I would never complain, Rebecca. Consider it a simple endearment, if anything." Kissing her on the forehead, he squeezes her bottom before pushing her toward the front door. "Now, let's get going."

They make it to the aquarium or the Under the Sea Discovery Centre a half hour before it closes, and just in time to catch the tail end of the final performance of the night for the octopus tank. After the octopus performance, they spend a few minutes handling the starfish, then head into the gift shop where Aiden buys her a big stuffed purple octopus. "Are you hungry?"

Bouncing on the balls of her feet, she takes his hand and pulls him out toward the street vendors. "I could use a hotdog."

"A hotdog?" He sounds as if she just asked him for an old tire.

"Yeah! Street-meat is awesome, come on."

"I was thinking maybe Haro's or the Waterfront Grill."

He shoves his hands in his pockets, stubbornly as they stand in front of the hotdog cart.

Tucking her arms through his, she wraps them around his waist and looks up into his eyes. "Loosen up, Baby. Try a hotdog, please."

A smile graces his kissable lips, and he nods. "Alright, only because you called me baby and on one condition." He leans in close to her ear and whispers. "When we get home, you let me see if that cute little ass of yours really is off-limits."

Wow! Okay, I was not expecting that condition.
"Aiden..."

"Now now, Rebecca." Giving her a stern look, he pulls his hands from his pockets and places them on her upper arms. "Tit for tat. You promised to open yourself up to try new things, and I'm agreeing to do the same thing by ingesting a hotdog."

Rebecca huffs. "Aiden, that's not even remotely the same! You're asking me to introduce a foreign object into a body cavity that's not designed to be violated in such a way."

Aiden chuckles at her. "A hotdog is a foreign object to my body and a violation of my digestive tract. It's exactly the same thing. What does it matter which end of the body it's going into? Besides, anal is quite common between two consenting adults."

Shifting her weight to one leg, she puts her hand on her hip. "I can't believe you just said that! Eating one hotdog will not hurt you. Stuffing your dick in my ass, however —" She takes a breath reminding herself they're in public. "I've heard that it can be rather painful."

The realization of her real fear flashes in his eyes, and his face softens. "Fine, I'll eat the damn hotdog. But I've told you a couple of times now, Rebecca. I would never hurt you." Taking her hand, he turns her toward the hotdog cart to place their order. "I know this is still really new between us, but you need to trust me." He smiles up at the vendor and puts two fingers in the air as if he has done it a million times. "Two, please."

She sends him a suspicious glance, and he shrugs. "I may enjoy the odd hotdog from time to time, but given the option of Haro's or a hotdog." He shrugs, smiling slightly with a shake of his head. "No one in their right mind except you baby would choose a damn hotdog."

She laughs, taking the hotdogs from the vendor. "I happen to like hotdogs." She squeezes mustard across them and hands one to Aiden.

Glancing at her, he smirks. "Yes, clearly."

Walking as they eat, they head in the direction of the pier. They pass the fish market and glass beach, stopping to take pictures with the famous wooden scuba diver, and a couple pictures with the statue of the old man sitting on the bench holding his lunchbox and flowers. A few couples are walking along the pier, and an older Chinese couple are crab fishing over the edge of one of the fishing balconies. Aiden takes her hand, leading her out to the end of the pier overlooking the open ocean. Aside from a couple of flashing lights marking random boats coming in and out of the harbour, you can't see anything. There's no moon or stars out tonight, making the sky appear pitch black. It's also much chillier out on the pier then it is onshore.

He leans his back against the rail, tucking her into his chest and wraps his warm body around her. "Are you cold?"

"I am a little."

"It's getting late anyway. Why don't we head back to the car?" Keeping her tucked close to his side, they head off the pier. As they near the last fishing balcony, she spots Alex and his drummer Johnny sitting on the bench. Lowering her head as they approach, she tries to pretend she doesn't notice them, but Aiden stops to point them out. "Hey, isn't that Alex and his buddy?"

"Yeah, I think so." She continues to walk, pulling him along with her. "I'm surprised he's still in town and even more surprised to see him out here. Can we just hurry up, please?"

Pulling her to a halt, he gazes down at her. "Hey, I don't

want you worrying about him, especially if you're with Max or me. I promise I won't let anyone hurt you." She lets out a squeal as Aiden scoops her up into his arms.

"Jesus, Aiden! I don't want him to know we're here. I've never seen him like he was today. That was scary," she says, swatting at his chest.

"Baby, I said I wouldn't let anyone hurt you." Even though she believes him, the last thing they need today is more drama. When they reach the edge of the walkway, Aiden sets her on her feet and spins her to face him. Resting his hand on the side of her neck, he gently sweeps his thumb across her cheek. "I mean it, Rebecca. You're safe with me."

Nodding, she meets his eyes. "I know. I just don't like conflict."

He kisses her forehead and takes her by the hand. "We'll always avoid it when we can. Now, what do you say I take you home so I can warm you up properly?"

She smiles up at him, but then suddenly, the thought of what will happen after 30 days plagues her as they head for the car.

Is it really enough time to make a love connection?

I know I feel like I'm falling for him, but

Is he even capable of true love?

On the way back to his house, she can't help but ask. He seems to be lost in his own thoughts as she peers over at him and lays her hand in his lap. "Aiden?"

"Mm-hmm."

"What's going to happen when the 30 days are up?" She lays her head against the headrest and faces him, watching for any signs that might give away his true feelings, but he keeps his eyes focused on the road ahead.

"What exactly do you mean, Rebecca? I thought I made my expectations very clear the other day during lunch." He turns to face her with a questioning glance. "Is there something specific you'd like to discuss?"

Feeling the heat creep across her cheeks, she shakes her head. "No, I guess not. I just wish there wasn't any contract between us, that's all."

He reaches into his lap and takes her hand in his. "Let's try and forget about the contract for now. Okay? Let's concentrate on the here and now. If things are meant to be, everything will all fall into place on its own."

With a nod, she gives him her best-forced smile. "Okay."

Max's Hummer is parked in the driveway when they arrive back at the house, and Aiden groans at the sight of it. He gives her an apologetic look. "I had no idea he was going to be here. I'll get rid of him."

"I don't mind him being here. He doesn't bother me." She smiles, recalling their banter earlier this afternoon. "I kind of like him. He brings out the real Aiden."

Aiden shakes his head. "I'm not convinced you'd like the real Aiden. I'm trying really hard to be different with you, Rebecca." With a quick kiss, he gets out of the car and kicks Max's tire. "But, this asshole is making it extremely fucking difficult."

Rebecca gets out of the car, laughing. "Do you feel better now?"

He throws his arm around her shoulder with a smile. "Yes. I do, actually." Giving the tire one more kick, he kisses on her forehead. "Ahh, okay. Let's go see what he wants. Shall we?"

Chapter 7 — Surprise!

As Max leaves Rebecca's house, one thought keeps running through his mind...

I'm done watching Aiden act all prim and proper. She's not one of our associates. How dare he have this little princess all to himself? I can feel it. She's the one we've always talked about - that one girl that can satisfy both our needs and still ask us for more. I can see it in her eyes, in her body language.

She's hungry.

She's the perfect mix of good and bad, and I need a fucking taste.

With the arrangements made, Max slips into his Hummer and heads over to Aiden's to spring his plan into action. When he pulls into the driveway, Aiden's car is gone. So, he lets himself in and slides on the pair of Lycra swim shorts he keeps there, knowing they show off his best assets. He dives into the pool to swim a few laps while he waits. As suspected, only a few laps in, and he lifts his head to see Aiden and Becca standing at the end of the pool waiting for him. He leaps out of the pool mere inches from Becca's side with a big smile. "Hey, guys! I got tired of waiting, so I thought I'd take a dip."

His smile broadens as Becca's stare trails across his body with a whole new intensity.

That's right, Baby.

I knew you were hungry.

Aiden raises his brow at Becca, tossing Max a towel. "We weren't expecting company tonight. Rebecca caught a chill down at the pier." He pulls her protectively against his chest. "I thought we'd have a warm bath and head to bed."

Max inwardly laughs at Aiden's greedy actions.

Yeah, great idea, but I don't fucking think so, bro!

Rebecca holds his arm and looks up at him. "Actually, I'm fine now, Aiden. Really. I warmed up on our way home in the car."

Max smiles at the sight of Aiden's jaw clenching.

Haha, I like this girl! That's obviously not what he wanted her to say.

Making sure he flashes Aiden his biggest shit-eating grin ever. Max slaps him on the back. "Great! Then get your swimsuits on and meet me in the hot tub. I have something I want to discuss with you both." He gives Becca a little wink. "You'll warm up in the hot tub anyway, Princess."

Aiden groans as he reluctantly releases her from his arms. "Fine, but this better be worth my sacrifice, Max."

Chuckling, Max heads for the hot tub. "Jesus, Aiden. Loosen the fucking leash a bit, will ya, bro!"

Earning him the flip of the bird as Aiden disappears into the house.

While they're changing, Max grabs some glasses and a bottle of champagne, making sure he has the envelopes close by to show them his surprise. He can't wait to see their reaction. Especially Aiden's when he tells them he's booked them a three-week vacation at one of the hottest adult resorts in Montego Bay.

Max sits in the hot tub and stews...

Aiden will know precisely what's on my mind. He doesn't know that I've seen his little contract yet, but he will. The fact that he didn't intend to ever share Becca with me that pisses me off. He thought I would be in Seattle the entire time and be none the wiser. Just for that reason alone, he's lucky I don't take her away and keep her for myself. He's lucky I'm a fair man. I don't mind sharing like we originally planned, but — now we do it my way.

The opportunities in Jamaica to bring our dream to fruition are plentiful, and no ex-boyfriend to interfere.

It's perfect.

Aiden nervously paces as he watches Rebecca slip into her bikini. He knows Max's intent. He knows Max was supposed to be part of the deal, but she's too perfect for sharing. He's afraid to lose her with a proposal that includes Max. She was timid enough with his own proposal. He also knows it's best to hear it from him then from Max. "Rebecca, there's something you should know," he says, running his hand through his hair. Something Rebecca has already come to recognize as a nervous or tense response. "Max and I have shared women many times in the past," he says in a low voice.

Her reaction is not at all what he expects. She doesn't pitch a fit or shy away. In fact, she barely acknowledges what he's said. Instead, she places her hand on her hip and draws her brows together. "That's nice to know, Aiden, but I didn't see your brother's name on our contract. So obviously, that doesn't apply to me. Now, does it?"

Aiden shakes his head. "No, you're right. I guess I'm just telling you this, so you know our history and understand when I ask you not to encourage his advances because it's becoming obvious to me that he will make them."

She exhales slowly and shakes her head. "I don't want to know about your historical bedroom games. Now please, let's go downstairs. I could really use a drink, especially now that you've just sprung this on me." She pulls him toward the door as if his words had no effect on her.

When they get out to the patio, Rebecca catches Max's eyes, following her like a tiger stalking his prey, and a sudden feeling of unease begins to wash over her. Quickly striding over to the hot tub, she wastes no time at getting in. She takes a seat directly across from him while Aiden takes his place beside her and lifts her legs onto his lap. Max holds out a glass of champagne to Rebecca and smiles. "Here, princess." He chucks his chin at Aiden and holds out another. "Here, bro. Try to fucking relax, will ya?" Max's gaze bounces between the two of them, and he raises his glass in the air to toast. "To Jamaica!"

His face lights up when Aiden and Rebecca look at each other skeptically. Holding up three travel packages, he lets out a hoot. "Woohoo! We're going to Jamaica bitches! I booked us reservations at one of the most exclusive adults-only resorts in Montego Bay! We leave in 2 days."

"What?!" Aiden and Rebecca say simultaneously.

Max laughs. "Yeah! You two are just gonna kick around here and have sex all day anyway, and you'll likely keep running into Becca's ex. This is perfect. It's not like you can't have sex in Jamaica, and when you come up for air, you can have fun with me!"

Aiden tilts his head, trying to decipher Max's true intentions. "Fun with you, huh?"

Smiling, Max raises his hands. "Yeah, Aiden. I'm actually

quite a fun guy."

He waves his hands toward Rebecca. "Besides, I like Becca. She deserves a real chance at happiness." He lifts his glass to Aiden and winks. "But, with this dick that dumped her suddenly coming back and trying to stake his claim. We need to take her away from this nonsense. She doesn't need that kind of bullshit. Anyway, I heard he's leaving town again in two weeks. We'll be in Montego Bay for the next three." He shrugs, taking a drink of his champagne. "Problem solved. Besides, I could use the holiday."

Aiden leans back, giving Max a questionable look. "You sure this isn't just a ploy to try and get Rebecca away from me?"

"Aiden..." Rebecca says, sounding a tad annoyed.

Max raises his brow at Aiden. "Look, I'll admit I'm a little pissed at you, but that's not what matters right now. Rebecca is a free woman. She can make her own decisions, and I'm here to make sure she does." Max directs his attention to Rebecca, completely ignoring Aiden. "Tell me, princess. Are you happy with Montego Bay?' Cause I can take you somewhere else," he says with a wink. "You know. We can leave the old man at home, and I'll take you anywhere your little heart desires."

Glaring at him, Aiden splashes water in his face. "Fuck you, Maxwell! I'm not sure what you have up your sleeve, but it better not include Rebecca."

"Lighten up, Aiden." He runs his hand down his face sweeping the water away. "Let's just go and have a good time. We've earned it." He rolls his eyes cracking a smile. "Okay fine, maybe you earned it more than me. Whatever! We're still going, and we're gonna have fun!" He yells so loud the vein in his neck visibly expands like an inflatable balloon.

With a wide grin, Aiden holds his hands up in front of him. "Okay, Okay! Just don't fuck with my lady." He shakes his finger at Max. "I'm not kidding, Max."

Max grins mischievously. "Shit! You're using your big boy words and everything. Wow, Becca. What have you done to my boy?" He shakes his head at her in disbelief. "As I see it. It can only be one of two things. You're either purely angelic, or you're the devil herself." Raking his eyes across her body, he chucks his chin. "So, which is it?"

Rebecca laughs nervously.

Nope. I am not biting this hook! You boys need to behave.

Looking between the two, she seems to be the only one laughing. Max appears to be waiting for a real answer while Aiden folds his arms across his chest and decides to give him one. Taking a deep breath, he puffs out his chest. "Actually, she's as pure as the undriven snow. At this point, we're making our own roads."

He looks at Rebecca and smiles. "Personally, I'd have to say we're building them somewhere between heaven and hell. Our journey so far has been pure bliss, if you must know."

Max stands with wide eyes and a slack jaw. "Wow, Aiden! That was fucking hot! Did you think that up all by yourself?" He stands and hands them both shooters. His face is still tense with expression as he stares at Aiden. "Seriously, when did you get so fucking sensitive, bro?"

Rebecca bursts out laughing. "God, Max! I need a brother like you."

I honestly do wish I had a brother or at least a sibling. I've always wanted one. I think having someone like Max to grow up with would have been fun.

Aiden throws an inflatable cushion at him, letting out a chuckle. "Shut up, man."

When the men finally settle down, Max hands them each a travel envelope. His gaze slides to Rebecca. "You do have a passport, right, Princess?" She nods, barely paying attention while checking out their travel information. "Good! Then we're set to go. We fly out the day after tomorrow." He grins at Aiden. "Oh yeah, I forgot to tell you. We're using the company jet. I had Natasha set everything up. Thanks for leaving her at my disposal. She's been amazing."

Aiden visibly tenses, and his eyes narrow at Max. "Okay, do not abuse Natasha. There is no possible way I could replace her. She could single-handedly run that company."

Rebecca's eyes shift between the two brothers. "Is this a joke? Are we actually going to Jamaica?"

Aiden pulls her into his side while Max lets out a chuckle. "Yes, baby. We are actually going to Jamaica. You know how you said you wished you had a crazy brother just like Max?" He throws his hand in the air. "It looks like he may have just claimed you." He glares at Max. "As his sister, that is. Right, Max?"

Max shrugs, as a grin takes over his face. "Oh, make no mistakes, princess. I am claiming you." He throws his arms out to Becca. "We're gonna make the best threesome!" His choice of words makes a shiver run down Rebecca's spine, as Aiden's words playback in her mind – 'Max and I have shared women many times in the past.'

Clearing his throat, Aiden gives her a reassuring smile, then pats her bottom and gives her a slight shove toward Max's open arms. "There's so much to teach you, little one." Max takes a deep breath and pulls her into a tight embrace. "You're gonna be so much fun to party with!" He kisses the top of her head. "You know it's official now, right? You're ours! It doesn't even matter what happens with Aiden. I'm keeping you."

Taking Rebecca's hand, Aiden pulls her back into his lap. "All right, all right. Let's get a few things straight. First off, threesome was a poor choice of words. She is clearly with me. Secondly, she is not ours. Again, let me remind you. She's with me."

A mischievous grin forms on Max's face. "Whatever you say, bro." He winks and pretends to punch Rebecca's shoulder playfully, rotating his hips and dancing the best he can in a hot tub. "Don't let him scare you. We can always ditch him. Aiden might run the show here, but in Jamaica, we do what we want. In fact, I think we may need rehab by the time we get home!"

"I can't wait! I haven't been this excited since I went to Cuba with my friends on spring break. It sounds like a lot of fun!" Rebecca gives him a quick hug. "Thanks, Max."

"Anytime, princess." He looks at Aiden with a grin. "Oh, I'm gonna need one of your spare rooms tonight." He puts his hand up before Aiden can say anything. "Don't worry. I'll take the one at the opposite end of the hall. I know you haven't had a chance to soundproof the place yet." Stepping out of the tub, he pats Aiden on the back. "Now I think I've earned steak and eggs for breakfast tomorrow. Don't you?" He rubs his rock hard abs. "I'm a growing boy, you know."

Shaking his head, Aiden smirks. "Yeah, I'll see what I can do."

"Thanks, bro." Throwing his hand up, he waves on his way into the house. "Night, Becca! Try and keep it down tonight, will ya?"

She smiles, feeling her cheeks heat. "Goodnight, Max! I'll do my best."

Rebecca is thankful Max is heading off to bed when Aiden hollers back. "Just for that, I'm going to make her moan and scream my name until you can't help but grab for the lube."

Max flips him the bird as he disappears through the doors.

Aiden rests his arm behind her head. "Well, there you have it. There's no denying Max likes you. I'm just not convinced yet it's all brotherly."

"I think you're reading more into it then there actually is." She holds out her hand to him, showing him her pruned fingers.

"I guess we should get you out of here before you grow scales." He kisses her cheek and gives her a nudge toward the steps. "We've had enough excitement for one day anyway. Don't you think?"

"Yeah, I definitely have to agree with you there."

~ ~ ~

Max stays with them at Aiden's for the next day and a half until it's time to leave, and the dynamics of the house is unmistakably one of a tight family unit. The three of them have become inseparable.

When it's finally time to leave, the guys load their bags into Max's Hummer, and they head for the private airstrip to board the company jet for Jamaica. Rebecca sits upfront with Max and fiddles with the radio when a station announcer sings out, "We have a new single from Alex Healey this morning. It's called Becca." The three of them grow quiet as the ballad from that first night, when Aiden had taken her to the bar, melodically begins to echo through the speakers.

The corner of Max's mouth lifts slightly as he changes the station. "You don't need to hear that, princess. He's a fucking dog."

He's absolutely right.

"You're right. Alex even said it himself. It's too little too late." A slight smile pulls at her lips as Aiden's reassuring hand lands on her shoulder. He reaches for her seatbelt and unbuckles it, gesturing for her to join him in the backseat. She climbs between the two seats landing in his lap, and wraps her arms around his neck. "I'm not going to let him or his stupid song ruin this. I've never been this happy." Her tongue sweeps across Aiden's lips as he sucks it into his mouth, taking her mind miles away from Alex Healey and anything they once had.

"Okay, you two lovebirds. As hot as that is to watch. There will be no fucking in my truck if I'm not involved," Max bellows from the front seat.

Aiden chuckles, giving her a quick smack on the bottom. "We're not fucking in your truck, but I am hoping I can convince Rebecca to join the mile high club today."

Rebecca laughs nervously. "Aiden!" Max glances back at them through the rearview mirror. He loves the way Becca's cheeks brighten instantly while Aiden simply shrugs it off matter-of-factly.

When they board the jet, Rebecca's amazed at the inside. It's like walking into an elegant mobile 1-bedroom apartment. There's a lighted partition that separates the dining and sitting area. On one side, four reclining chairs surround a dining table at the front when you first enter. On the opposite side of the glass partition, there is a sofa facing a credenza and flat-screen TV. Just beyond that is a bathroom, which is nothing short of spectacular. It's certainly nothing like on a commercial flight and even larger than her bathroom at home. At the very back of the plane is a bedroom with a full queen size bed and another built-in TV. They literally have all the luxuries of home on this plane.

She turns to look at Max and Aiden with wide eyes. "This

thing is amazing! It's like a flying apartment!"

Aiden smiles and pats Max on the back. "Yeah, it was a good call for this trip. It will be a comfortable 7-hour flight."

Max's grin is one of total satisfaction. "I've got everything covered, bro. You'll see. I even ordered a prime rib for dinner. We're gonna have a fucking blast!"

The pilot steps onto the plane and salutes. "Morning, gentlemen. Are you about ready to take off?"

The rest of the crew consisting of three other people, walk in behind him and smile, taking their positions. Two head into the cockpit and one into the small kitchenette.

Max slaps his hand on the arm of his chair. "Andre, good buddy! We're more than ready! Take us to the fun in the sun!"

With a big smile, the pilot turns toward the cockpit. "Danielle will serve drinks once we reach altitude. As usual, I'm going to ask that you stay buckled up until then."

The jet engines roar to life, and within a few minutes, the plane is racing down the runway picking up speed for takeoff. Aiden takes Rebecca's hand and kisses it. "I'm pleased that you're here."

She lays her head on his shoulder. "Me too."

When the pilot announces they've reached altitude, Max unbuckles his belt. He's decided he's not waiting for Danielle. Grabbing a bottle of whiskey and three glasses, he sets them down on the table with a wild grin. "Let's get this party started!"

Pouring them each a shot, he lifts his eyes to Rebecca. "You know, I think you're pretty special, right?"

Nodding, she accepts the glass from his hand with a warm smile. "Thanks, Max. That means a lot. I think you're really great too."

Handing Aiden his glass, he returns her smile. "Good, then I'm going to make myself clear. I personally don't give a fuck whether you're with Aiden or not. If you need someone for any reason, you can call me, day or night." He gives Aiden a stern look. "I'll be there. And I will hurt anyone that tries to hurt you. I don't care who they are. I promise."

Rebecca can feel herself choking up. No one has ever cared that much for her before, at least they've never voiced it. She can also tell Max's words are not sitting well with Aiden right now. "Aww, Max. That's one of the sweetest things anyone has ever said to me. Thank you." She clinks her glass to his and swallows her shot, placing her glass back on the table. "I desperately need to pee before I add any more liquid to this body. Excuse me a minute." What she needs to do is remove herself from this conversation quickly. Aiden looks edgy, and Max seems to be ticked off at something.

As she's closing the bathroom door, she overhears Max talking to Aiden in an angry tone.

"Aiden, don't be a fucking dick. Just give her to me. I'll treat her right for the right reasons." Max sounds more pissed with each word he speaks.

Aiden chuckles. "You're just pissed I tried to exclude you. I have no intention of hurting her or letting you have her, Max. Rebecca and I have some things to discuss when the times right."

Max swallows his shot and slams his glass down on the table. "Come on, bro. I saw the fucking contract. You're going to set her free after 30 days. I know you. That makes you a major fucking idiot. Look at her. She's not in this for the money. She truly wants to be here. If you were smart, you would destroy that contract and put a ring on that girl. If you don't, I gladly will. Have you even discussed our original plan with her at all?"

Wait, what original plan? And, I'm sorry, but did Max just say he'd marry me?

Rebecca clears her throat and shuts the door harder than necessary to let them know she's coming. "Hey! Do either of you know how to make slippery nipples?"

Both men instantly spin their heads toward her with their eyes wide. She swears as though Aiden just gulped when Max suddenly bursts out laughing. "Fuck, princess. My heart stopped for a minute!" He slaps Aiden on the back. "Relax, old man. It's a fucking shooter. She stunned me for a minute too."

Oh, shit! Whoops!

Giggling, she snuggles up to Aiden. "I'm sorry. I just realized how that must have sounded. Max is right. It's a shooter. I think it's Bailey's and Sambuca."

Max ducks behind the bar and starts sorting through bottles of alcohol. "You got it, babe." He slams two bottles down on the bar, a bottle of Sambuca and a bottle of Bailey's Irish cream. "I'll give you a slippery nipple, or anything else you can think of for that matter. Just say the word."

Rebecca can see Aiden's nostrils flare when he glares at Max. "Okay! I don't want to hear you say you're going to give her a slippery nipple. I am certainly not a prude. I know it's a drink, but Jesus, Max, I know what you're suggesting, and you're coming on a bit too strong!"

Rebecca kisses his cheek. "Baby, he's just trying to get you going."

Max sits three shot glasses on the table and bellows as

he raises his glass. "To the nipples, I intend to make slippery in the next three weeks! And I'm not talking about drinks!" He clinks his glass with theirs.

Aiden stares at Rebecca with a wicked smile. "I have no problem making your nipples slippery."

"God! It's just a damn drink! You two are such men!" Rebecca downs her drink and slaps her glass on the table for effect, but when she quickly sucks in air through pursed lips, the effect is quickly lost to laughter.

Max laughs, giving her a wink. "I'd say one more of these, and you should be just about ready for an orgasm."

She bursts out laughing as Aiden's face turns red. He picks up a magazine from the rack alongside the table and heaves it at Max's head. "I'm not fucking with you, Max! That's enough!"

Grabbing Aiden's arm, she tries to control her laughter as she wipes the tears from her cheeks. "Aiden, you let him get to you so easily. It's just another shooter." She laughs. Aiden looks skeptical, but he doesn't often frequent bars. "I'm serious. It really is a shooter. They're Kahlua, Amaretto and Bailey's." She looks over at Max for confirmation. "Right?"

Max laughs as he nods. "Yeah, you're right, but you should have let him stew on that one a bit." He chucks his chin in

Aiden's direction. "I know I'm gonna."

Wiping his hands with a damp towel, he winks at Rebecca and smiles. "Anyway, I'm going to go check on dinner. I don't know about you two, but I'm getting kinda hungry."

Aiden shakes his head as he watches Max disappear into the kitchenette then turns his attention back to Rebecca. He lifts her chin with his finger. "You thought that was pretty funny, huh?"

She shakes her head with a chuckle. "Oh, come on, Aiden. He's just toying with you."

Kissing her, he takes her hand and gently pulls her from her seat. "I'm not convinced he is, but he's not my concern at this moment. Let's go to the bedroom. I'll show you what I put into an orgasm."

"Ohh, I like these lessons." Following him into the bedroom, she jumps onto the bed. "At least turn on the radio or something. We don't need Max hearing us this time."

Turning on the TV, Aiden strips off his clothes, tossing his t-shirt at her playfully as he crawls onto the bed. "I really don't care if he does." Rebecca giggles as she starts to slide off her miniskirt when he stops her. "Leave it all on."

Reaching his hand up her skirt, he pulls off her panties, tossing them to the floor. Slowly sliding his hand up the inside of her leg, he stops just above her knee and pushes them open. The light caress of his fingertips circling their way up her inner thigh sends goosebumps rushing to the surface of her skin. She lifts her hips, trying to add more pressure to his touch, but his hand closes around her thigh. "Stay still, baby."

Letting out a frustrated moan, she relaxes back into the bed. Using his slightly splayed fingers, he moves gently over her inner thighs toward her mound and slides his body up alongside hers as one of his fingers traces its way over her slit. She reaches her hand out to touch him, but he shifts his hips back just out of her reach. "Not yet."

"Come on, Aiden. I want to feel you."

"Mm-hmm. You will. I promise." His finger slips between her folds, brushing her wetness up and down over her swollen bud. There is no way for her to remain still any longer. The rotation of her hips are now involuntary as her hand reaches out once again, finding him close enough to seize his solid manhood. She swipes her thumb over the tip collecting his wetness, and spreads it around the head before gently stroking, matching the rhythm of his finger. He leans in, and the warmth of his breath feathers across her chest only moments before the heat of his tongue hits her flesh. "God damn it, baby. I need to taste you."

Her mind begins to protest at the thought of losing his tantalizing touch, but her stomach fills with excitement, knowing there is so much more to come with his offer. She reluctantly releases him from her hold with a groan, and he quickly straddles himself above her. "Don't look so disappointed. We're not done yet."

He lifts her tank top and cups her breast in his hand, covering her pebbled nipple with his warm mouth. When he releases it, he looks down at her with a teasing grin. "Now, that's a slippery nipple. Tell me, baby. It's been a while since I've been on a bar spree. Is there a shooter called the satisfied clit?"

Shaking her head, she bites her bottom lip in anticipation watching as he slides down her torso. As his head disappears between her thighs, she can feel his warm tongue slide through her folds. He places a hand on each of her inner thighs, pressing them open and sucks her sensitive bud into his mouth. A carousel of excitement floods her body. Her back instantly arches, and her hands fall to the back of his head, clutching his hair to pull him closer. "Oh – My - God!"

Fantastic fireflies dance under her eyelids as her legs begin to tremble. "God, Yes, Aiden!"

A lustful moan escapes her lips as she grabs him by the hair, pulling him up to face her. "Let me try returning the favour for a change."

His face lights up when she pushes him onto his back and shimmies down his body.

"Baby —"

She looks up from between his legs. "Shhh, if you don't like it, I'll stop."

Laughing, Aiden peers down at her. "Oh, I can assure you. There is not a chance that I won't like it."

A drop of pre-cum glistens as it slides down the head, urging her to take a taste. She wraps her thumb and forefinger around the base, cupping his balls in the palm of her hand. Her tongue sweeps out, licking the droplet off the tip as her mouth closes over the head. A deep moan rises from Aiden's chest as he watches his shaft disappear into her mouth. Rolling her tongue around him, she can feel every ridge as she makes her way back up to the tip. He grips the bed sheets, fisting them in his hands while the length of her tongue circles the head. Slowly she works her way back down until she can feel him hit the back of her throat. She swallows to allow him passage, and his hands fly to the back of her head, holding her still with a deep groan. "Fuck, baby! If you don't stop, I'm going to cum."

She raises her eyes to meet his and slowly releases him from her mouth with a smile. "It's okay. I want you to."

Without another word, his eyes roll back in his head, and he lies back with a moan. Running her tongue along the large muscle underneath from the base to the tip, she circles the rim before sinking her mouth back over his shaft.

With his balls cupped in the palm of her hand, Aiden's hips lift and lower, pushing himself deeper into her throat with each stroke. She can feel him start to swell, and his hand once again slides through her hair. His body begins to tense, and his voice strains as he jolts. "Holy — Fuck, Baby!"

A blast of warm salty liquid hits the back of her throat, and she swallows just in time for a second burst to fill her mouth. She can feel the pulse against her lips and wonders if it matches the rhythm of his heart as he labours to breathe. Aiden takes a deep, cleansing breath and reaches down, lifting her face to look at him. "Come on up here." When their lips meet, he moans into her mouth. His kiss is as intense as his release. "My god, Rebecca. We may need to discuss that contract."

Gazing down at him, she grins. "Oh, really?"

Wrapping his arms around her, he kisses the top of her head, exhaling through partially pursed lips. "Yeah, I'm afraid 30 days may not be enough for me." He tightens his grip with a growl. "Let's go get cleaned up before dinner."

After their shower, she pulls on a clean skirt and tank top then heads out to the main cabin where Max is watching a movie. He smiles up at her, and instantly she feels herself flush. She's waiting for his taunting, but this time Max seems different. His eyebrows draw together, and he shakes his head. "Don't be embarrassed, princess. It's a natural, instinctual need." He switches off the TV and stands. "Dinner is ready. Danielle was just waiting on you two." He gently strokes the back of his hand across her cheek and gives her a chaste kiss. "I'll let Danielle know you two are ready."

Aiden walks over to join her at the dining table and laces his hand through her hair, pulling her head back for a kiss.

It's a completely savage move!

And I fucking love it!

Sigh —

"Thanks." He runs his hand down the side of her face. "I should've said that before you left the room. I'm sorry." Smiling, she remembers the look on his face after he came. That was all the thanks she required.

Max flops down across from them and grins. "So, what were you two doing in there?" he asks, waggling his eyebrows at Aiden.

Shaking his head with a slight smirk, Aiden takes a drink. "Drop it, Max. We were just talking."

With a mischievous grin, he stares at Rebecca to gauge her response. "Maybe next time you should include me in your little talk. I have some great insights."

Aiden grits his teeth and glares at him. "Max. Knock it off."

Chapter 8 – Jamaica

Thankfully, Danielle wheels out the dinner cart, interrupting the brothers' banter. Dinner looks amazing, consisting of prime rib with gravy, roasted potatoes, and baby carrots. Max opens a large bottle of red wine and pours them each a glass. The guys seem unusually quiet during dinner, so Rebecca decides to break the ice. "What time will it be when we arrive?"

"I think Andre said we'd be arriving around 9 pm their time. Don't worry. We'll still have time to hit the bar. In fact, it really doesn't matter." Max drops his fork and wipes his mouth, pulling out his travel envelope from his bookbag beside his seat and hands it to Rebecca. "I booked myself in the presidential suite. It's perfect for after-hour parties. Oh, and you two are booked into the master swim out suite. You have your own hot tub and pool." He finishes refilling their wine glasses and settles back down in his seat. "We can party all night if your little heart desires, princess. My room never closes."

Aiden closes his eyes and rubs his forehead. "Perfect. This is going to be three weeks of partying for you two, isn't it?" He studies Rebecca's face closely as a smile forms on her face.

God, Max is right. She's perfect. She's sweet and innocent when necessary but yet still wild, crazy and adventurous. She is everything we've been searching for. I just don't know if I can share her.

Max clinks his glass against Rebecca's. "Abso-fucking-lutely, bro! Join in or back the fuck off! No buzzkills allowed. Right, Becca?"

Rebecca smiles with a nod. "I kind of have to agree, Aiden. You have zero worries here. No one knows you. When we leave in three weeks, we'll never have to see them again." She stands and raises her arm in the air. "Try that crazy-named drink! Just eat that fucking hotdog, Aiden!"

The two of them burst into laughter while Max raises his brow in question as he watches.

Still smiling, Aiden clanks his glass with theirs. "You're right. We're here on vacation. I'll try to loosen up a little, but I still need to be the voice of reason here. After all, someone has to make sure you two don't get yourselves into trouble."

Max thinks about that for a minute. "Uh, we're going to be at an all-inclusive adults-only resort. We can't possibly get into trouble. So again, lighten the fuck up, bro."

"I get it, Max. Don't worry. We're going to have a good time." He finishes his wine and excuses himself, heading for the washroom.

Andre announces they will be landing a half-hour earlier than expected, getting them into Montego Bay at 8:30 pm. Max and Rebecca cheer, startling Aiden as he opens the washroom door. He takes a bow. "Well, thank you. I've been doing it all by myself since I was about two. It's really not that big of a deal anymore."

Rebecca laughs. "We weren't cheering about your peeing skills, silly. We're almost there, and we're going to be early."

Chuckling, Max pats him on the back. "But I bet your peeing skills are pretty boss too, bro."

There's a limo waiting to take them to the resort when they land. Their chauffeur is a tall, dark Jamaican gentleman with a slender frame, wearing a suit that is at least two sizes too big for him. He never stops smiling, and no matter what Max or Aiden says to him, he smiles and says, "No worries."

However, the most startling thing is when he hands Max a joint as he opens the back door to the limo. "Here you are, Sir. Compliments of the resort."

Aiden shakes his head. "Oh, that's real classy, Max. What kind of resort is this again?"

Laughing, Max holds his hands up in defence. "Come on, Aiden. This is Jamaica, it's known for its weed. It's just an adults-only resort. No one under the age of 21 will be here." He winks at Rebecca. "That makes you just barely legal little one."

Rebecca shrugs. "That sounds like more of a reason for me to celebrate. Don't you think?"

Pulling her into his side, Aiden chuckles. "Jesus, Max. You're creating a monster."

As soon as the limo starts moving, Max lights the joint. He takes a couple of drags and hands it to Rebecca. She's never smoked weed before, but when in Jamaica...

She glances over at Aiden to get his approval, but he merely shrugs. So she takes a drag and nearly chokes half to death. Aiden rubs her back, trying to stifle his laughter while Max breaks out into full roar. "Damn, princess. You're such an amateur. Here." He passes it back to her. "Don't take such a big drag."

She takes a small puff this time, and Max holds his finger over her lips before she can exhale. "Perfect. Now, hold it in."

When she does finally exhale, her head spins for a brief second, and she has to blink several times to refocus. Max passes it back to her and again reminds her. "Go easy. Little puffs."

Taking a drag, she holds it in this time without being prompted and passes it back to Max.

Grinning, he reaches for the joint. "Ah, you're a quick learner."

When she exhales, she can feel the high making its presence known.

Oh my god, I am sooo high. Shit. Did I just say that out loud? Pfft, it doesn't matter. Wait, am I laughing in my head, or can they hear me? Oh, I'm not sure if I like this feeling. My lips feel like they're being held hostage in a huge grin. Hehehe, that's kind of funny. Damn, did I eat dirt?

Max looks over at her and points, his head falling back with laughter. "Shit, princess! You are so stoned! You should see your perma-grin!"

The look of Max cracking up alone sets off her own laughter. She looks over at Aiden, trying to focus on him through her tears. The hope that his serious face will help settle her giggles is lost as soon as he lays eyes on her and starts laughing. "Wow, baby. He's right. There is no denying it. You are unmistakably high."

When they arrive at the resort, they are an absolute laughing mess. Their driver opens the limo door, and it must look like a bad Cheech and Chong movie to anyone standing by to witness it. Smoke barrels out the door as it opens and Aiden steps out, watching as the two of them file out, trying desperately to contain their laughter and remain on their feet. Aiden holds his hand out to Max. "I think you should give me the itinerary. I'll deal with the reservations."

Still laughing, Max reaches into his pocket and pulls out the paperwork for their reservations and hands them to Aiden. "I think that might be a good idea, bro."

Aiden chuckles, giving Max a slap on the back as he takes the papers from his hands. "Yeah, me too."

Turning to hand the itinerary over to the gentleman so concierge can prepare their rooms, Max leans his big body against a statue, believing it to be a pillar. The statue tips and falls to the ground, smashing to pieces. All that can be heard is Max's loud voice echoing through the main entrance. "Oh shit!"

Bending down, he tries to pick up the pieces as a couple of the staff members rush over to help. "Fuck! I'm really sorry," he says, fighting back his laughter.

Rebecca is rolling with laughter while Aiden tries to explain that they don't usually smoke weed but indulged at the driver's urging. The concierge has obviously dealt with this kind of thing before. He simply nods with a smile. "It's no worry, Sir."

Another gentleman graciously waves them forward to escort them to their rooms when Max gives him an odd look. "Dude. Where are our bags?"

"Yes, Sir. They are already in your rooms. Please, follow me." He turns, waving them forward as a gesture for them to follow him.

Max looks at Aiden with a deadpan stare. "Holy shit! He didn't say no worries!"

Rebecca is still trying to recover from the statue incident when she bursts into laughter once again. Aiden smacks him on the back, trying his hardest not to react. "I think that was all for entertainment. What do you say we just follow him to our rooms, huh?"

Weaving their way through the resort, they finally reach the backside by the open coves. The gentleman stops and opens the first door to a large, beautifully decorated suite. He turns around, his eyes questioning between Max and Aiden. "Mr. Maxwell Collins. The Presidential Suite, Sir."

Max takes the key card from his hand and waves. "Thanks. I can't believe they don't allow you guys to accept tips." He walks inside and hollers. "Woohoo! You two come get me once you get settled in!"

Rebecca and Aiden follow the gentleman a little further down the path to the next door. He slides the key card through the lock and opens the door, holding out his arm. "Here you are, Mr. & Mrs. Aiden Collins. The Master Swim Out Suite."

Aiden knows it's likely an assumption on the concierge's behalf, but he actually likes the ring to that. He quickly looks over at a questioning Rebecca and smirks as he takes the key from him. "Thank you."

As soon as the door closes, Rebecca shifts her weight to one hip and tilts her head up to look at him with a sideways smile. "So, I'm Mrs. Collins here, am I?"

His arms wrap around her as he chuckles. "I'm sure it was a simple assumption. Although it does have a nice sound to it, don't you think?"

Not waiting for a response, he kisses the top of her head and takes her hand. "Let's check this place out."

Their room is massive and beautifully decorated. The open concept is airy and inviting. There is a small kitchenette immediately to your right as you walk into the suite that houses a microwave and refrigerator along with a couple of other small appliances, it's quaint, but it's definitely the smallest part of the unit. The living room is large, with finished concrete flooring made to resemble deep gray marble. All the walls are white except for one. An accent wall on the left is tiled in black glass and has a built-in flat screen and a full-length ribbon fireplace. A black microfiber sectional faces the floor to ceiling window doors that retract entirely into the wall to reveal a step-in hot tub and swim-up pool. And just beyond the fireplace wall is a king-size bedroom with a sizeable double soaker tub set into the corner window. The bathroom is completely done in long multi-tone grey stone. It's equipped with an oversized master shower that has an added waterfall head and doubles as a sauna. There's a small room joining the bedroom and bathroom that holds the sink and toilet. Rebecca is lost in amazement, knowing this suite must have cost a small fortune when Aiden wraps his arms around her, pulling her from her daze. "This is a pretty spectacular room. Max really has outdone himself."

Nodding, she looks up at him and smiles. "This is truly amazing. We have to go see his room. He has the presidential suite, and he said he has the party room!"

Shaking his head, Aiden groans. "God, what has he done to you?"

Dragging him along with her, she heads next door to Max's room. Aiden knocks and opens the door taking the lead. The decor is all very much the same, but Max's suite is twice the size of theirs, occupying two full floors. There's a balcony off the living room upstairs that overlooks the ocean and, of course, Aiden and Rebecca's pool. There's a dance floor beside a small bar area on the lower level, fully equipped with a disco ball and spotlights. Large column speakers stand in every corner that run all the way up to the second floor for the sound system. He wasn't kidding. This really is a party room.

Max hollers from down the hall. "Hey! Come check this shit out!"

Following his voice, they find him in his bedroom, which is twice the size of theirs with a king-size bed and a walk-out terrace that overlooks their hot tub. The bed nestles against the wall at one end of the room while at the far end, he has a hot tub and a minibar. His bedroom alone is a party room. Rebecca's mouth drops open. "This is amazing! How did you find this place?"

He shrugs, leading them back out to the rest of the unit. "I researched the best adult-only resorts." His kitchen is a full kitchen with full-sized appliances and a dishwasher. "This was rated the best in Montego. So, I booked it."

Aiden pats his back. "You really have outdone yourself, brother."

Max disappears into his room and comes out in a fresh pair of black shorts and a white t-shirt. "Let's go check out the bar."

They follow the path and the music leading to the bar. Rebecca can see Aiden is finally loosening up as they dance along the pathway to the music. As they get closer, the music gets louder, and all at once, they recognize the song. Simultaneously they yell out, "One Love!"

Rebecca grabs hold of Aiden and Max, pulling them along excitedly. "Oh my god. I love Bob Marley!"

Trying to keep up with her, Aiden laughs. "Baby, I think you love everything right now. Are you sure you're not still high?"

Walking into the bar, it's not busy at all. A few people are dancing, and there are a couple of people at the bar, but it's certainly not as active as they expected. They walk up to the bar, and Max asks the bartender where everyone is. The gentleman smiles, and in a thick Jamaican accent, says, "At di beach fa di welcome tradition." He points toward the beach. "Yuh muss guh or it be bad luck, yuh know." He hands them each a towel and shoos them off. "Yuh muss guh now."

Max claps his hands. "Well, we don't want any bad luck now, do we. Let's go!" Nodding with a smile, Aiden takes Rebecca's hand and follows Max toward the beach. As they approach, they spot a bunch of nude bodies dancing about near the waterfront with a low-lying cloud of smoke lingering just above them. From the overpowering smell of weed wafting through the air, the chances of it being from the small bonfire are slim to none.

Clearing his throat, Aiden halts Rebecca. "I don't think this is the right place."

Grabbing his arm, Max tugs him forward, giving him a stern look. "Yeah, I'm pretty sure it is. Let's ask someone." He heads over to a naked lady that has clearly had a bit of something to smoke and gets her attention. "Excuse me, darling. Is this the welcoming ritual?"

Running her hands down his face while she dances in place, she gives him a toothy smile. "Yep, it is. Damn, you're a handsome one, aren't you?"

Giggling, she reaches for his shirt. "You have way too many clothes on, honey. Let me help you."

Aiden's eyes grow wide. "Well, this is a different type of welcome."

She spins, her eyes locking onto him with a moan. "Ohh, am I seeing double again? Here honey, let me help you get undressed."

Backing up, Aiden shakes his head. "No. No, I'm fine."

Staring at Aiden and Rebecca, Max takes off his shirt in his usual devil-may-care manner. "Fuck it! What can it hurt? Everyone else is naked. Come on, take it off. We're going in the water, and it's dark anyway."

With a stern look in place, Aiden eyes Rebecca. "Don't you dare, Rebecca."

Feeling a little brazen, she snickers, toying with the hem of her tank top. "Aiden, it's a tradition. I don't want bad luck while we're here." She gives him a pleading look and pulls her tank top over her head, tossing it at him.

"Woohoo! That a girl, Becca!" Max yells, cheering her on.

"Rebecca." Aiden's voice hardens, dripping with a warning.

Max laughs. "Come on, bro. Pull the stick out of your ass and take your clothes off."

Reaching for the clasp on her bra, she joins Max in coaxing Aiden to strip down. "Come on, baby. I need you, or I'll have to hold onto Max when we go into the water. I'm afraid to touch the bottom."

A mischievous grin forms on Max's face as he stares over at Aiden. "No problem, princess. I'll gladly carry you in."

"Like fuck, you will!" Aiden bellows, stripping off his shirt and tossing it at Max's head. "You knew this was a thing, didn't you, Max?"

Still laughing, Max shakes his head. "Nah, bro. But it's fucking great. It's like getting a fucking detailed menu."

"Yeah, fucking great." Aiden drops his shorts as Rebecca pulls off her skirt and panties.

Taking an eyeful, Max whistles. "Holy fuck! You definitely found a keeper, bro." He darts for the water in his naked glory.

Aiden lifts Rebecca into his arms and strides for the water. "Jesus, Rebecca, you could drive a man insane." He cradles her close to his chest while dunking them into the warm Caribbean water, staying only long enough to ensure they've gotten wet.

Tossing her over his shoulder, he leaves her ass in the air as he walks them back into shore to get dressed.

Dangling down his back, she smacks his bottom in protest. "Aiden! You can put me down now. We're onshore."

Running by, Max smacks Rebecca's ass leaving a stinging sensation that both hurts and sends waves of excitement through to her core. She yelps, reaching back to put her hands over her bottom with a chuckle. "Damn it, Max!"

"Let the games begin, little one!" He watches the glow of his handprint appear on her ass.

God, she's perfect.

As Rebecca is slipping her skirt back on, she looks up and catches a glimpse of Max's naked glory. Taking a moment to appreciate the perfect male form before her, she allows her eyes to travel from his muscular calves all the way to his eyes. The very same eyes that are staring back into hers. He gives her a sly smile and does up his shorts. "I'm gonna go scope out the bar. Are you two coming or what?"

Rebecca's shocked when Aiden speaks up. "Yeah. I guess we may as well. We just went skinny dipping with all these people. I'd say we're kinda like family now."

The bar still isn't packed, but there are definitely more patrons present than there was before.

Max saddles up alongside the bar and pats the barstool beside him. "Come on, princess. You can sit beside me." He waves his hand at the bartender and hollers with three fingers in the air. "Three Bob Marley shots, a gin and tonic and two Jamaican rums straight up, please."

The bartender smiles with a wave signifying he's heard him. Aiden stands beside Rebecca with his arm wrapped around her waist and his lips at her ear. "We'll just have a couple of drinks, and then we'll go back to our room." Giving him a slight nod, she thinks a swim in their private pool and possibly a replay of their first night together sounds pretty hot.

The bartender no sooner places their drinks on the bar in front of Max when he hands Aiden and Rebecca theirs. Max raises his glass high. "Cheers! To the three of us, may we have many new adventures in Jamaica!"

"Woo!" Rebecca hollers, clanking her glass with his and Aiden's before downing her shot. She slides her empty glass back to Max. "Another!"

She feels Aiden's hand tighten around her waist and hears Max laugh. "Yeah!" He waves at the bartender for another round. "We'll have another round of Marley shooters, boss!"

Waving back, the bartender acknowledges he's heard him and begins mixing their shots. Before Max can lower his arm, a sexy dark-skinned beauty locks her arm around his and plants herself on the stool next to him. "Hey, honey. Are you looking for a good time?"

He looks her over at her in disgust and laughs. "Sugar, I'm having a good time, and it's already paid for. Now get your dirty paw off me before I call over the resort security."

Scowling back at him, she huffs. "Well, you definitely aren't as friendly as you look, are you?"

"Yeah? How's this for friendly? Fuck off, bush pig!" He shoots her a disgusted look and spins to face Rebecca and Aiden.

Rebecca gives him a curious look. "That was a bit harsh, Max. I thought you wanted to find women."

He laughs. "Princess, you don't know what you're talking about. That was not a woman. That was a prostitute. I will never be that desperate. Besides, I already have my eye on a woman."

Aiden chucks his chin at him with a smirk then kisses Rebecca's cheek. "Drink your shot, baby. Let's go dance."

She downs her shot and pats Max on the arm. "Oh. Well, then. Good choice. You don't want to take home any dirty pussy." Winking at him, she slides off the stool and into Aiden's arms.

"Cute, princess. Real cute!" Max slugs back his rum and motions to the bartender for another.

They head out to the dance floor as Zayn sings Pillowtalk. It has a seductive rhythm, and Aiden loves to grind, on and off the dance floor. Lifting her arms, she slowly lowers them over his head, kissing him softly as he runs his hands down the sides of her body to her hips. Her splayed hands run down his chest, caressing the hefty bulge of his pecs when he suddenly grips her hips and spins her around — jerking her back so her backside presses against his groin. He rolls his hips into her bottom until her hips move with his. She raises her arms, reaches back to hold the nape of his neck while he runs his hands along her sides. "Mmm, I love the way you dance. I would never have guessed you were such a good dancer." She closes her eyes and lays her head back against his chest, savouring the feel of his delicate touch. His lips brush against her collarbone. Laying light kisses along her neck and he releases a low growl next to her ear.

"There's a lot you don't know about me, Rebecca."

"I'm sure there is." She closes her eyes again, letting the beat of the music move their bodies. When the song fades to the classic Bump and Grind by R. Kelly, she feels a second hard body form against her. A leg presses its way between her thighs, and her eyes shoot open to see it's Max pressing firmly against the front of her. "What are you doing, Max?"

She can feel Aiden's chest shake against her back as he laughs. "We're doing what the song says, baby. You can't tell me you've never done the bump and grind before."

Holy shit! Is that a drummer playing between my thighs? Having these two grind their groins simultaneously into me is shrouding my thoughts. Okay, I know I should stop Max — but I honestly don't want to. Why am I not pushing him away? Oh god, my hips seem to have a mind of their own.

"Mm-hmm, but you said not to encourage Max," she says, still allowing her body to do as it pleases while her mind bathes in alcohol and ecstasy.

The heat of Max's tongue sears the flesh between her breasts as it slides across her collarbone to her neck. His lips are soft when they brush against her ear. "Trust me, princess. He didn't mean what he said."

And the drummer picks up his pace, playing a master's solo between my thighs.

Aiden cups her breasts and breathes heavily into her hair. "Shh, you can relax, baby. I've seen the way you've been looking at him. Besides, you told me to loosen up and honestly, we're just dancing."

Oh my god! Is this really happening right now?

The song comes to an end, and Max slowly backs up, never losing eye contact with her. Shaking his head, she hears him make a low growling sound as he kisses her hand. "Thanks for the dance, princess." He glances at Aiden. "You need to change your mind before I stop being so fucking brotherly."

Leaning in, he kisses Rebecca on the cheek and heads back to his stool at the bar.

Turning to face Aiden with a look of confusion, Rebecca wraps her arms around his neck. "Change your mind about what?"

"Don't worry about it. He's been drinking." He pats her bottom and points toward the bar. "Let's go have a drink."

When Rebecca takes her seat beside Max, he glances over at her with a smile. He slides a shooter in front of her and nudges her elbow with his. "Drink up, Princess. There's another round coming."

Aiden sits down next to her, sipping his rum while seemingly deep in thought. Max slides another set of shooters down to them and holds his in the air, grinning. "To dirty dancing. May there be much more where that came from." With a wink, he downs his shooter slamming his glass down on the bar. "And, on that note. I'm gonna call it a night before I start some shit. I'll see you two kids in the morning."

Rebecca turns as Max leans over to kiss her cheek and catches the corner of her mouth. His eyes flick up to meet hers, and her cheeks begin to burn. "Goodnight, Max."

He shakes Aiden's hand and knocks fists with him. "Goodnight, bro. Tomorrow for sure."

Aiden shrugs. "We'll see." He looks at Rebecca and chucks his chin at her empty glass. "You ready to call it a night, baby?"

She slides onto his lap and runs her tongue across his lips. "I'm ready to go back to our room."

"Mmm, now that's what I like to hear." Grabbing hold of her waist, he tosses her over his shoulder like a sack of potatoes. Her hands slap off his back in protest as she giggles and hollers at him to put her down, but he laughs, ignoring her as he continues carrying her to their room.

He tosses her onto the bed and hovers over her. His cobalt eyes look deep into hers as he slides his hand up her skirt. "Did you leave your panties at the beach?" She nods with a chuckle. "No wonder you were so worked up while we were dancing tonight."

"In my defence, they were full of sand, and how was I to know I would be sandwiched between two of the hottest twin brothers I've ever met. Besides, I told you I hate clothes, remember?"

He removes her skirt with one quick yank and tosses it to the floor.

"That you did, baby. That you did." He flops down beside her with a grin and trails his hand along her stomach, slipping it under her tank top and lifting it over her breasts.

The light touch of his fingertips tickle, and she jolts upward with a giggle, grabbing his hand, pulling him over her. "Aiden, stop teasing me."

He shoves her back with a groan. "I like teasing you." His tongue circles her nipple before sucking it into his mouth and releasing it with a loud popping noise. Lifting his head from her chest, he begins to move down her body with a wicked smile. "Mmm, I've wanted to do this all night."

His head drops between her legs, and his tongue slides between her folds, eagerly stroking her sensitive bud.

All Rebecca can think — is heaven.

Her back arches, and an erotic moan escapes her lips. "Oh, Aiden!"

Hearing her pleasure shifts him into the next gear. He slides his hands under her knees, pushing her legs up to her chest and, with an animalistic groan, buries his face deep between her thighs. She jolts with the aggressive contact as his mouth covers her entire mound, but as his tongue slides back through her folds, delving into her opening, her back arches and her mind blanks. "Holy shit, Aiden!"

The only thing that is present in her mind at the moment is the sensation that's rapidly blooming from her core. Everything else seems so insignificant right now. It simply doesn't exist. When she vaguely hears feral moans, she prays her ears are deceiving her. They can't be coming from her mouth, but when Aiden pulls her swollen bud between his lips and sucks like a Hoover – no amount of praying could say otherwise. It's her making that noise.

She's just too far gone to care what she sounds like.

Shit! Are those fireworks?!

Her muscles tense as waves of excitement wash over her,

and her thighs begin to quiver. "Oh – My — God Aiden!"

He releases her legs and looks up at her, licking his lips with a smile. "Yes, baby. That's what I like to hear. Now, open up and let me show you how good I can grind now that we're alone."

Alcohol and exhaustion are slowly taking over as she sprawls open with a slight moan. "Mmm. I'm so done." Suddenly, her mind floats back to the earlier commotion on the dance floor, and she pictures herself sandwiched between Max and Aiden. The heat and the lust of the moment completely overpowering her actions.

When Aiden grabs her bottom, grinding into her as deep as he can, he instantly brings her thoughts soaring back to him. His grip tightens, and he plunges into her, rolling his hips.

Once.

Twice. He slowly grinds. "Holy fuck!"

He thrusts

Once.

Twice. A slow seductive grind. "Oh — my — god baby."

He groans, lowering his lips to hers, swallowing her moan before it escapes. He continues his thrust and grind delivery until they are both left completely sated and drained. He literally fucked her until exhaustion put her to sleep, and him too.

Rebecca wakes the next morning to Aiden withdrawing himself from her body. Her eyelids flutter open to his smiling face. He kisses her forehead and jumps out of bed. "That's a first for me."

"You slept inside me all night?" She snickers at the thought of it, throwing on Aiden's t-shirt as she heads for the bathroom.

He shrugs, patting her bottom as they pass each other. "Yeah, I guess I did. I would have taken advantage of that position this morning if Mother Nature didn't insist her call was answered first. I'm good to go now, though, if you're interested."

Good to his word, Aiden's lying sprawled out naked on his back when she walks out of the bathroom. Giggling, she lies down beside him. "You're ready now, are you? That's funny. I think I recall you being the one who called me insatiable. Do you remember that?"

Running her hand across his chest, she watches his manhood spring to attention. "Oh! Yes, you are ready." Biting her lip, she wastes no time climbing over to straddle him, but just as she leans down to kiss him, someone knocks on the door. Her head jolts back up, looking behind her as Aiden groans and pulls her back down.

"Ignore it. It's probably housekeeping. They can come back later." Their lips meet once again, and they hear another knock, only louder and accompanied by Max's deep voice. "Stop fucking and open the door!"

Aiden growls as she breaks their kiss, rolling off him with a chuckle. "You better answer him. You know he's only gonna get louder if you don't."

"Damn it! He can be a real pain in the ass." She can feel the frustration ripple off him as he pushes himself off the bed with a groan. Stabbing his legs into a pair of boxers, he heads toward the door.

Max's boisterous voice echoes through their suite as he walks in the door. "Jesus, do you ever get off her, bro?"

Quickly covering her mouth with her hand to stifle her laugh, she can picture Aiden running his hand through his hair with a smile when she hears him spit back. "Are you seriously asking me that right now? Would you?"

Rebecca slips on her bathing suit and heads for the living area to find Aiden and Max in the middle of some crazy handshake until Max spots her. He chucks his chin at her and smiles. "Morning, princess. Are you going for a swim before breakfast?"

"Yeah. I'm hoping it will wake me up."

"Mind if I join you?" Stripping off his shirt with no concern for her response, he tosses it on the sofa and looks back at Aiden with a wink. "Why don't you order us some breakfast, bro. I could really use some steak and eggs benny."

Rebecca waves at Aiden from the pool. "Oh, me too! Please, baby."

Diving into the pool, Max swims up next to her and leans against the ledge. "You looked pretty hot last night, rolling your hips between us. I almost think you wanted more."

Feeling herself flush, she looks into the room for Aiden. "Max," she warns.

Reaching out, he rests his hand on her hip. "No, seriously. I mean it, Becca. That was the hottest thing I've seen in a long fucking time." He licks his lips. "I woke up, still tasting the sweat from your cleavage."

Holy shit! Did he really just say that?

She reaches up, putting her hand on his chest to keep him at a distance. "Max, I don't think Aiden would be pleased if he were to walk out here right now."

He tugs on the string of her bikini bottoms and releases them from her body with a feigned look of shock. "Shit. What happened? Do you think he'll be pissed now?"

Gritting her teeth, she tries to snatch her bottoms back

from him, but he holds them high above his head, using his 6'4" frame to his full advantage. "Come on, Max! That's not funny!"

"Aw, come on. I saw you naked last night at the beach, remember? You have no reason to cover up now." His eyes drop, looking down into the water at her nakedness before they slowly travel back up to meet hers with a crooked grin. "If Aiden is stupid enough to actually let you go, I plan on making it my goal to make you mine." He shakes his head. "Nah, you know what? Fuck it. I don't care if Aiden thinks you're his or not. He hasn't married you yet. That makes you a free woman in my books."

She can hear Aiden's deep voice before he even walks out onto the patio. "Max! What the fuck are you doing?"

Still holding her bikini bottoms in the air, Max turns to face him with a shit-eating grin. "Oh, Becca lost her bottoms, and I just wanted to help her put them back on, but she's being difficult."

Aiden doesn't look overly amused as he stands across from them, folding his arms over his chest. "Why can't I help but think you had something to do with them getting lost in the first place? Now, give her back her bottoms."

Keeping them high above his head, he smiles at him. "Of course, bro. That's what I've been trying to do." Turning back to face Rebecca, he winks and blows her a kiss. "I told her to come to get them." A mischievous grin slides across his face. "Aren't you going to come and get them, princess?"

Rebecca looks up at Aiden with begging eyes, but he shrugs with a smirk. "I just got dressed, baby."

"Are you kidding me? Really, Aiden?" She brazenly raises her brow at him. "Okay. Fine." Taking one last look at her obstacle, she charges forward, climbing Max's body like a jungle gym. With her bikini bottoms in hand, she feels like she single-handedly won a round of capture the flag.

Both guys look so stunned that neither one looks as if they are even breathing. With an enormous smile on her face, she slides back down Max's chest with her bottoms in hand. "Yes! I'd call that a victory!"

Aiden's jaw has come completely unhinged. Likely from seeing her girlie parts mashed against Max's face.

Good! Maybe he'll do something next time.

She's not honestly sure Max even knows for certain what just happened. He kind of looks confused. Pointing at Aiden, she raises her brow. "Don't look so shocked. You should have gotten them for me." Turning to face Max with her own well earned shit-eating grin, she says, "And you...You should've been prepared, big talker."

Max's eyes grow wide as he snaps his mouth shut and swallows. A broad smile forms across his face as he shakes his head. "You are so right. I wasn't ready, princess. Any chance I can get a do-over?"

Rebecca laughs, shaking her head. "Yeah, that's going to be a no, Max!"

Staring at her in wonderment, Aiden holds his hand out. "Jesus, baby. You never cease to amaze me."

Tying her bottoms back on, she reaches to take Aiden's extended hand. "Seems you may be open to sharing me with Max after all, huh?" She waits for Aiden to deny it, but he doesn't. Instead, he leans down and gently kisses her cheek.

That was kind of a proverbial punch to the gut. That's fine. Good to know — GOOD TO KNOW!

Forcing a smile, she grabs her towel, heading for their room. "How long before breakfast is here? I'm going to get dressed."

He hollers back to her from the patio. "It should be here in about 5 minutes or so."

Throwing on a pair of Lycra shorts and a dry bikini top, she adds a touch of liner and pulls her hair up into a messy bun. Aiden opens the door and peeks in. "Breakfast is here, beautiful."

"Okay. I'm coming." Shutting off the TV, she follows him out to the dining table.

Max holds his fist out. "Fuck, Becca. You rock! The more I replay that whole scenario — the hotter you look on my face."

She laughs, smacking his fist away. "Max, you didn't even know what hit you."

"Oh, you may have stunned me, but I know exactly what hit me," he says with a sly grin.

Throwing his hands out, Aiden yells. "Okay! We all know what happened out there."

He waves his hands in the air and looks at each of them. "Are you done? — How about you, are you done? — Good."

Breakfast is almost finished when Max speaks up. "Oh shit, I almost forgot with the whole Becca sitting on my face ordeal, but we're supposed to be down in the spa at eleven for the total package. We're booked for mud-baths, massages, facials, pedicures and hair treatment. Four hours of pampering. Doesn't that sound like heaven?"

Raising his brow, Aiden leans back in his chair with his coffee. "Facials and pedicures?"

Max shoves a whole slice of bacon into his mouth and licks the grease from his fingers. "Hey! Don't knock it until you try it."

"I think it sounds wonderful. I've never had a mud-bath before. After all, it's all about new experiences. Right, Aiden?" Rebecca can't help but throw that in any chance she gets.

Folding his arms, his chest rises and falls with an inflated breath, his lips pull into an uneven grin, and he nods. "You're absolutely right, Rebecca." He swipes his hand out to stop any further discussion. "But, I'm gonna have to draw the line at the makeup and polish."

Max bursts out laughing. "Hey, that's your loss."

He checks the clock and slaps his hand down on the table. "You can decide when we get there. We gotta go."

Chapter 9 – Quality Time

The spa has both indoor and outdoor facilities. Built amongst a palm grove, it's entirely private both inside and out. When they walk in, the first thing they notice is the palms that grow naturally through the thatched roof. Max gives their names, letting the receptionist know he has booked the family package, and they take a seat to wait.

The receptionist or she could be a masseuse; with their nondescript uniforms, it's difficult to tell. It's one of the things Rebecca has noticed since they've arrived. Not one of the workers could be defined from another based on their uniforms at this resort. All the wait staff, housekeeping, the bartenders, and the maintenance crew, even the souvenir shop attendant wear the same uniform. Either way, this young woman rocks her outfit. She's a beautiful dark-skinned lady in her late 20's, and from both men's reactions, you can tell they're hoping she'll be the masseuse.

With a bright smile, she summons the three of them to follow her through the reception area and out to the semi-enclosed deck outside where the relaxing trickle of a stream that runs under the wall gives a feeling of superior tranquillity. Three rather large stone tubs sit side by side filled with a grayish coloured mud, each adorned with rolled towels at the end for a pillow. It's likely the most beneficial yet least appealing room in the entire spa.

The attendant tells them to strip down, giving them each a pair of thin fibre underwear to wear. "Yuh war only dis," she says before leaving the room.

Rebecca quickly surmises Jamaica to be quite open sexually when the attendant thinks nothing of leaving them all in the same room to change. It doesn't seem to bother Max either. He doesn't skip a beat stripping off his shorts and pulling on the thin piece of fabric to hop into his tub. "Oh yeah! This feels like heaven." He looks up at Aiden and Rebecca curiously. "What are you two waiting for? Get in!"

Aiden stands, blocking Rebecca's body while she turns her back toward Max to slip into the flimsy panties. Glancing over, Max shakes his head. "Princess, I told you I've already seen it. Besides, Jamaica is not a place to be bashful. We're gonna have to work on that tomorrow when we go to the nude beach where clothing is not an option."

Aiden steps into his tub between Rebecca and Max and takes her hand. "She's not all that bashful. One of her biggest assets is that she hates clothes."

She chuckles, recalling the look on Aiden's face the night she stripped off her dress in his car.

Looking at Aiden with a dumbfounded glare, Max shakes his head. "I see, so Aiden just has you afraid to get naked around me then."

Shooting daggers at Aiden, Max nods knowingly. "I'm happy to know it's not you, princess."

He knocks Aiden's fist. "Well played, but I don't think that's gonna work, bro."

Rebecca has no idea what Max is talking about, and Aiden suddenly seems to be miles away, concentrating on running his fingers across her hand. She's not even sure if he's heard Max at all. Time to try to lighten the mood. "Well, I happen to think I'm pretty damn lucky right now. I'm sitting here with the two hottest guys at this resort."

Aiden doesn't say anything. He just squeezes her hand with approval and smiles.

"Woo! That's right, princess!" Max lifts his hand in the air, unintentionally flicking mud at Aiden. Of course, knowing these two, it just might have been intentional.

"You know, I wouldn't be able to tell you two apart if Max got his hair cut and his beard trimmed," she says, pointing out the apparent differences.

"Well, you're in luck, princess. I'm getting a shave and a haircut today before we leave this building," Max says with a wink. "Oh, by-the-way, I saw a tattoo parlour in the brochure. We could all get some ink as a souvenir to remember our trip."

Scooping up a handful of mud, Rebecca rubs it across her arm. "I've always wanted a tattoo! I'll get one!"

"A tattoo Rebecca?" Aiden chuckles, "I'm pretty sure Max is talking about the permanent kind."

She gives Aiden a perturbed look, glancing past him at Max. "Sign me up, Max. I want a tattoo." Aiden shakes his head when she glares back at him. "You know the permanent kind."

Max claps his hands together with a hoot, sending mud flying in all directions and laughs.

Okay, that time, it was definitely intentional.

"That's my girl! I'll book us all an appointment tomorrow. If Aiden wants to be a bitch and chicken out, that's on him."

Wiping her hands with the cloth at the side of her tub, she glances between Aiden and Max. "Oh! I almost forgot. I saw a billboard outside that said a cover band would be performing Bob Marley and Marvin Gaye in the main dance hall tonight. We should check them out."

Aiden's eyebrows raise in question. "Baby, Marvin Gaye and Bob Marley are both dead."

She gives him a dirty look. "I know he's dead, silly. It's a cover band."

"Fuck yeah! Marvin Gaye? Like, Sexual Healing Marvin Gaye? Oh, shit yeah. Count me in! That spells bump and grind in our dance world."

Max Stands, swinging his muddy hips as the curtain to their deck opens, and two beautiful ladies come through with a tall, dark mountain of a hunk. The women walk toward Aiden and Max, asking them to follow them to the showerheads along the opposite side of the deck while the tall, dark wonder holds his hand out to Rebecca.

"Good afternoon, my name is Micah. I'll be your masseuse for today. If you could come with me, miss, you can get rinsed off right over here. Then I can take you for your massage."

Aiden and Max simultaneously let out an audible groan at the sight of Micah, the dark God of massage oil. Of course, Max can't help himself. There are times Rebecca swears he suffers from Tourette syndrome. "Hey, Princess. No happy endings, okay?"

Clearly, Aiden is annoyed and swats him in the arm. "Christ, Max. Just shut up!"

Micah smirks, holding up a robe to Rebecca. "I'll follow you to the shower so you can rinse, then you can slip this on, and we can head down to the massage tables."

He glances up at Aiden and Max with a smile. "It's a family massage room. The three of you will be together. I do hope you'll all be happy with the end results, but I'm afraid it will not be the happy ending you may have meant, Sir."

Rebecca rinses off and steps into the robe Micah is so kindly holding open to her then follows him into the massage room. The room is set-up with three tables, mellow island music is softly playing in the background, and the lights are dim with candles burning around the room to provide a light smell of jasmine in the air.

Aiden and Max are already lying on their cots face down with a sheet draped across their bottoms when Micah gestures for Rebecca to hop up onto the empty one. "If you could lie face down, please. We'll start with your back. Do you need a hand up?"

She shakes her head, wondering how she'll achieve it without baring all, but Micah quickly answers her question. Standing behind her, he opens her robe, letting it drop to the floor, then quickly replaces it with a sheet around her bottom. He pulls it under her arms and gathers it in front of her breasts. "Just hold it here and climb up," he says casually, proving he's done this a billion times before.

"Thank you." She climbs onto the cot and releases a slight moan as Micah's big hands press firmly into her flesh.

Max's voice rumbles from across the room. "Hey, Princess. If you need gentler hands, let me know. I'd be happy to take his place."

Aiden lifts his head slightly at her moan but only to address his brother. "Shut the fuck up, Max."

The massage is glorious, and at some point, Rebecca falls asleep. Of course, she only realizes this as a deep voice beside her ear wakes her. "Baby, it's time for our pedicures."

Her body snaps up to a sitting position before she's fully conscious, and she just barely misses smashing her head into Aiden's. "Shit! I can't believe I fell asleep."

Laughing, Aiden pulls up her sheet. "Relax. It's just time to move on to our next appointment. I've even decided to join you two for the pedicures."

Max places his hand on his hip and winks. "You can be honest, Aiden. You don't trust me alone with your woman."

"That may have something to do with it," he confirms, helping Rebecca up.

Heading off to the changing area, they dress and meet back in the main reception where the pedicure stations are. The pedicures, like everything else so far today, are simply amazing. When they're finished, the guys choose to wait for Rebecca before heading over to the hair salon. They sit sipping on rum while she has her toes airbrushed with palm trees. With pretty toes and the men satisfied from the rum, they head over to the hair salon down the hall for their final stop. Aiden and Rebecca only ask for a light trim while Max directs the stylist to give him the same cut and manicured beard as Aiden.

Aiden chuckles. "Getting the big boy haircut, Max?"

Stifling her laugh, Rebecca decides it best to say nothing. She can't wait to see the final result. They're already challenging to tell apart at a quick glance.

Max shrugs with a grin. "Gotta grow up someday, right? Besides, it's been a long time since we've sported the same do."

Heading off with their individual stylists, Rebecca gets her hair washed, trimmed and styled. The stylist applies some makeup and lets her choose from a wall of different perfumes. This is the true spa treatment if you've ever had one.

She's pleased with the results. Her skin feels incredibly soft, and it looks absolutely radiant. Her hair has been straightened, allowing her natural highlights to shine through as it cascades over her shoulders, just the way Aiden likes it. Her makeup is light, not overwhelming, as some salons prefer to apply it. In fact, the stylist has done nothing more than add a tint of colour to her natural beauty. The stylist walks into the back room, allowing her a few minutes to examine her final look on her own, then returns, handing her a garment bag. "Here, dear. Your boyfriend has asked me to have you wear this."

Rebecca opens the garment bag and finds a gorgeous red silk dress. It has a large oval neckline and diagonal mesh strip that wraps around the entire length of the dress, just missing the vital areas. It's classy, sexy and very daring. A shoebox attached to the garment bag produces a pair of red stilettos. They're not fancy, but they're perfectly matched to the dress. Once she changes, she takes one last look in the mirror. Rebecca's shocked at her own appearance.

When she opens the door to the main reception, Rebecca's facing true identical twins. She has absolutely no idea which one is Aiden. They're wearing matching suits and sporting identical haircuts. Their facial hair is trimmed to match. Who does she go to?

Then suddenly, one of them speaks. "Fuck, Becca! You just gave me an instant chub!"

She thinks...

Bingo! I found Max!

Laughing nervously, she walks into Aiden's arms, giving him a warm kiss. Glancing back at Max, he gives her a strange look as Aiden lets out a deep chuckle and spins her back to lock his lips with hers. A pair of arms wrap around her from behind. "Okay, that's enough! You win, Max. Let her go."

Fuck! They just played me!

Stepping back, she looks up into the smiling face of the man she was just lip-locked with and deflates, burying her head in her hands. "Oh, shit! You two seriously look identical now."

She turns to face Aiden with her cheeks burning and buries her face in his chest. "When you spoke like Max. I thought..."

Laughing, Aiden runs his fingers through her hair, an action she's become familiar with. Finally, she knows she's in the right arms. "It's okay, baby. Max just wanted to test it out."

Max casually strolls by with a grin. "Thanks for the kiss, princess. It was hot. I may have more of that later." He slaps Aiden on the back. "Let's go for dinner. I'm starved. What's this swanky place called again?"

"It's called The Papaya, and it has a 5-star rating in the

fine dining section of the resort brochure. Their menu looks fantastic." Aiden hands Rebecca his phone with the menu open. "Have a look at their menu."

She takes his phone and checks out the menu, pretending not to have heard Max's comment about having more of that kiss later. "Mmm, it does look good." She hands Aiden back his phone and slips her arm through his, continuing in the direction of the restaurant. "So, we just choose a menu plan then, and the courses keep coming?"

"Yep. I chose one for us when I booked our seats. We'll be having the calamari and grilled shrimp skewer starters, Caesar salad, and steam lobster with grilled asparagus and rice pilaf." Aiden glances down at her for her approval.

She nods her head. "That sounds amazing. I'm starved too."

When they reach the restaurant, the hostess approaches and Aiden immediately takes charge. "Collins party, please."

She nods with a pleasant smile and motions for them to follow her. The restaurant is upscale with plush seating and fish tanks used as dividers between dining areas. The tables are set with fresh white linen and more spoons and forks necessary for dining, at least as far as Rebecca and Max are concerned. The hostess leads them to a table in the far corner of the restaurant set for three, with an ice bucket beside the table already chilling a bottle of wine.

Aiden pulls out the centre chair for Rebecca and tucks her in, leaving the two seats on either side of her for Max and himself.

Once everyone is seated, Aiden pulls the cork on a white citrus flavoured Chardonnay and pours each of them a glass. Within minutes the dinner courses start coming.

The calamari is so tender they melt in your mouth, their batter providing just a hint of lemon as it hits your tongue. Rebecca could devour them all night, but as the calamari plates are removed, plates containing two garlic shrimp skewers take their place. The appetizers seem to be an endless stream when they come to collect the dishes and place small bowls of caesar salad down in front of them. Rebecca is almost full when the main entree finally arrives. A large plate with a freshly steamed lobster, grilled asparagus and rice pilaf is set down in front of her, and she leans back with wide eyes. "Where do you expect me to put all this?"

Aiden laughs, pointing at Max with his fork. "I had to be sure the growing boy had a full stomach before we go dancing."

Suddenly, Rebecca remembers the cover band at the main dance-hall tonight. "Oh, I hope we didn't miss the Bob Marley and Marvin Gaye show!"

Max rolls his eyes, cracking into the claw of his lobster. "You know we're in a Jamaican resort, right? We must have heard One Love at least ten times since we've been here already, Becca. We're never too late to hear any of his music, and I'm sure if you request anything by Marvin Gaye, they'll play it. Now, just relax and enjoy your meal."

They're all completely gorged by the time they leave the restaurant. Aiden puts his arm around her shoulder and kisses the top of her head. "Well, shall we see if we can still catch that cover band?"

Rebecca nods her head excitedly. "I'd really like to."

Sliding up beside them, Max pats Aiden on the shoulder. "Sure, let's go see if they can sing like the real Marvin and Marley."

They decide to head back to their rooms and change into something a little more comfortable before they head over to the dance-hall. Rebecca slips on a pair of Lycra shorts and a tank top while the guys put on a pair of black shorts and a white t-shirt keeping up with dressing alike.

Unfortunately, when they reach the main dance-hall, the cover band has already turned the show over to the DJ, but they're ready to dance, so it really doesn't matter. Max spots a free table beside the dance floor and leads Aiden and Rebecca towards it. Aiden again offers her the seat between them while Max calls the waiter over and orders a round of vodka shooters with beer chasers. When the shots arrive, Max automatically asks for another round. Aiden takes his glass and raises it with a simple statement. "To us."

Raising their glasses to meet his, they swallow their shots.

As the waiter brings the second round of drinks, Max raises his glass. "I think this is what you meant to say, bro."

He glances at Aiden before staring into Rebecca's eyes. "To the three of us. May we always be thick as thieves."

Clinking his glass with Aiden and then Rebecca, he slams back his drink and sets his glass on the table.

"You two seem different since the spa. What have I missed?" Rebecca says, pointing an accusatory finger between them.

Passing a look between themselves, they smile mischievously. Aiden reaches for her hand. "You haven't missed anything, baby. We've just agreed that we're here to enjoy ourselves for the remainder of our trip. Moving forward, there'll be no holds barred."

Max smiles slyly at Rebecca and slaps his hand off his knee. "Yeah! Let's test that. Shall we, princess?"

Waving the waiter over, he orders three lemon drops.

"What's a lemon drop?" Rebecca asks curiously.

Aiden eyes Max and grins. "It's just a shooter. I'm honestly surprised you haven't heard of it. You've done tequila shots before." She nods. "It's the same kind of thing but with vodka, lemon, and sugar. Max just likes to get up close and personal when he does them."

The shots are delivered to the table along with a plate of lemon wedges and a dish of sugar. Standing beside Rebbecca, Max looks down and smiles. "Okay, princess. Lick your lips." Grabbing a pinch of sugar, he dabs it along her moistened lips. "Let me demonstrate how this is done." Holding the lemon wedge to her mouth, he presses it against her bottom lip. "Here, hold this loosely between your teeth."

Rebecca sends a questioning glance at Aiden, watching as he smiles with a reassuring nod. "It's okay, baby. It's just a shooter."

She lets Max place the lemon wedge between her teeth and stares up into his eyes as he straddles himself over her lap. "Now, this happens pretty quickly. Are you ready, princess?"

Rebecca looks up at him with curious anticipation and nods. Max licks the sugar from her lips, quickly biting the lemon wedge from between her teeth and tips back the shot of vodka. His hand slides around the back of her neck as his lips cover hers. The sting of vodka fills her mouth, and she swallows as his tongue sweeps out, providing a hint of sweetened lemon to ease the burn.

Rebecca's mind warps momentarily, he looks like Aiden, but his kiss is more intense and much more demanding. She pulls away, watching him suck the lemon wedge from his lips with a lazy blink and a satisfied grin. "Damn, princess. Your mouth is so sweet there's no need for sugar."

Looking at Aiden, she waits for him to explode, but he doesn't. Instead, he stands and motions for Max to move, taking his place on her lap. Rebecca is speechless as he dabs some sugar on her already moistened lips and places a lemon wedge just as Max had done only a few moments ago. She looks up into his eyes as Aiden shoots back the shot of vodka and lowers his mouth to hers. Dislodging the wedge from her lips, he sweeps his tongue across hers with a moan.

Holy fuck! Not quite the same approach, but I like it.

He pulls back with a wink leaving Rebecca to lick the remaining sugar from her lips. "Mmm, I have to agree with Max. There's definitely no need for the sugar."

As Aiden lifts himself from her lap, Max takes her hand, pulling her to her feet.

"Come on over here." Placing his hands behind her thighs, he gently coaxes her to straddle his lap. "It's your turn, princess. You've been given two methods. You can use either one."

Rebecca smiles nervously as she glances at Aiden. "Uh, I'm not sure. Aiden…"

He nods. "You're fine, baby. It's just a shooter." He dips a lemon wedge into the dish of sugar and hands it to Max. "Here, we'll make it easier on you."

Max places the wedge between his lips while Aiden hands her the shot of vodka. Swallowing the shot, Rebecca leans down for the lemon as it disappears into Max's mouth. His tongue slides across hers, and she sucks it into her mouth, desperate for the taste of the sweetened lemon. His hands grip her ass, pulling her into him, and for a brief moment, she forgets this is Max. When her haze clears, she breathlessly pulls back, searching out Aiden's eyes behind her. Fully expecting to find anger, Rebecca is shocked when she's met with arousal instead.

Nodding with a smile, he holds his hand out to her. "Good job, baby. See, that wasn't so bad." He pulls her onto his lap as she watches Max remove the lemon from his mouth.

Aiden takes her hand and rests it against his swollen groin. "See what you do to me?"

Rebecca stares at him and shakes her head in confusion. "I don't understand. You enjoyed watching me make out with your brother?"

When his hand lands on hers, he smiles. "I told you this was something we've practiced, Rebecca." Briefly scanning her face, he shrugs. "Max is right. I've been selfish. I'm sorry. To prove my sincerity, I've destroyed our contract and had Natasha transfer the remaining $150,000 into your account. As far as I'm concerned, your commitment has been fully met. Your choices are now your own. You can choose to stay with me, or as I'm sure you're aware, Max is also interested in you." He takes a deep breath, glancing over at Max. "I'll let you know that we're not opposed to you dating both of us if that's your desire. Worst-case scenario for Max and me, you'll decide to remain on your own. Either way, the choice is solely yours now. You're a free lady again, Rebecca."

Rebecca feels an instant loss and instinctively shakes her head. "As silly as it may sound, I'm not so sure I want to be free."

Aiden can't hide his smile. "You're still mine if you choose to be, Rebecca. But from this point on, everything we do is solely your decision."

The song Mine by Bazzi echoes through the speakers, and Max takes Rebecca's hand, dragging her onto the dance floor. It's a seductive song, definitely a song Max wants to make her feel. Her eyes search out Aiden as Max snugs up against her backside, running his hands over her body while he sings the lyrics into her ear.

Lifting her arms behind his head, he lets his hands fall across the front of her chest to her hips

You so fuckin' precious when you smile

He pulls her hips into him, forcing her bottom against his groin

Hit it from the back and drive you wild

Wrapping his arms around her waist, he holds her snug against him and slowly grinds his crotch into her ass

Girl, I lose myself up in those eyes

Running his hands up her sides, he pushes her arms back up around his neck

I just had to let you know you're mine –

When she spots Aiden, he looks completely focused on their every move. He gives her a slight smile scanning the length of their bodies before settling his gaze back to the sway of their hips.

Max doesn't seem the slightest bit bothered by Aiden's presence as he continues touching her as if he owns her. He repeats his motions while his lips brush against her earlobe as he sings.

His hands slowly caress her breasts and slide down her sides to her hips

Hands on your body, I don't wanna waste no time

He licks along the side of her neck and drops his hands to the sides of her thighs

Feels like forever even if forever's tonight

Scraping his hands up her thighs to her hips, he grips them tightly pulling her against him

Just lay with me, waste this night away with me

Grinding his groin into her ass

You're mine, I can't look away, I just gotta say

With a sudden motion, his arm wraps around her waist, as he places the other hand between her shoulders and bends her forward, rolling his hips repeatedly against her behind

I'm so fucking happy you're alive

Swear to God, I'm down if you're down all you gotta say is right

Spinning her back around to face him, his mouth instantly falls to hers. His hands move to her ass, pulling her so tight to him that his arousal presses into her stomach and she can feel her core begin to throb.

The song ends, but before Rebecca can pull away, she feels another hard body press against her backside and hears Aiden's deep voice rumble next to her ear. "Jesus, Baby! I wish you could see how fucking hot you look."

He brushes the hair from her neck. "Max is going to add bubbles to his hot tub. We're gonna go relax in there for a bit and have a few drinks. We'd like you to join us. Okay?"

Nodding, she looks up at Max's smiling face as he takes her hand. "That a girl, princess. Let's leave your inhibitions here tonight."

Chapter 10 – A Quick Turn of Events

On the way to Max's room, she stops. "Wait. I've gotta grab my swimsuit."

Taking her hand, Aiden gives her a reassuring smile. "You're not going to need that, baby. It's just the three of us, and there's going to be bubbles. Besides, you hate clothes. Remember?" He winks and gently tugs her forward towards Max's suite.

Letting them into the suite, Max turns on some music and heads upstairs to the private hot tub in his room. After adding some bubbles, he makes a pitcher of vodka and orange juice, then calls down to Aiden and Rebecca to join him.

When Rebecca enters his room with Aiden directly behind her, she gives Max a questioning look. "Aren't you gonna get in shit for putting bubbles into the hot tub?"

Max shrugs with a crooked grin. "I'm not worried. That's why the room costs so much. They expect us to do shit like this."

Aiden suddenly spins her towards him capturing her mouth with his. Instinctively his hands drop to the hem of her tank top, lifting it over her head, and she feels Max slink up behind her. With quick hands, Max unsnaps her bra, and his hands slide around to cup her breasts. She glances up at Aiden as both excitement and nervousness wash over her. It's all she can do to keep her eyes glued to his.

He notices her looking a little uneasy, and glances down at the hands caressing her breasts. "You're okay, Baby. I'm right here."

His mouth moves across her neck, trying to recapture her attention, and she drops her arms allowing him to finish sliding the bra from her body.

Max's hands travel down her sides to her waist, and he slides his hands down the front of her shorts, pushing them down her thighs. Leaving her naked between them, he slowly backs away, pulling off his shorts and climbs into the hot tub with a deep breath. "Ahh, this feels amazing! Come on in here, princess." He waves her in toward the tub. "Come join me."

She can feel his eyes on her as she steps into the hot tub and feels her cheeks start to heat. Taking a seat quickly, she swipes a handful of bubbles across her chest and looks over at Aiden, watching him strip down and climb in beside her. Max hands her a drink and watches with amusement as Aiden pulls her onto his lap, having to quickly grasp her by the waist to stop her from sliding off. "Shit, Max. What the hell did you use in here? It's like we're in a tub of oil."

He is chuckling as he moves to sit next to them. "It's just regular bubble bath, but you're right. It's pretty slick." He reaches his hand out to Rebecca. "Come and sit with me, princess."

She glances back at Aiden as he takes her glass and nudges her towards Max. "Go ahead. I'll put your drink down and pour us each a shot."

"There you go, bro. It's good to see you've loosened up a bit."

Max pulls Rebecca onto his lap, guiding her back against his chest and slinks his hand between her legs, smoothly introducing a finger into her warm body. With a slight moan, she presses herself into his hand. She may have been caught off guard, but it's certainly not an unwelcomed touch. "Yeah, that's it, princess. I could tell you've been waiting for me to touch you all night. Haven't you?"

"Mm-hmm." Rolling her head towards Aiden, she can see him watching them. His pupils look dilated as he stands in front of them, holding shots of vodka in his hands.

"Okay, take a breather and let's have a toast." Kissing Rebecca, he hands them each a shot. "To us, and a night we'll never forget. May the memories last forever."

Max raises his glass. "Here here!"

Clanking their glasses together, they slug back their shots. Aiden once again seals his lips over Rebecca's, tangling his tongue with hers and pulls her towards him. Max quickly slides up behind her, pressing his hard member against her opening. She turns to look at him. Her lids heavy, she licks her lips, and he can tell she's just given him the okay to proceed. He grasps her hips, gently pushing forward as he guides himself into her warmth. When Rebecca releases a moan, Aiden's mouth reconnects with hers.

Max places his thumb against her puckered entrance, watching his manhood slide slowly in and out below. Massaging gently, he continually increases the pressure of his thumb with each stroke. She moans, trying to pull away from Aiden's mouth, but he holds her head, deepening their kiss and recapturing her mind.

Her thoughts start running rapid, and she can feel her heart rate increase. That's when Max's smooth voice seeps into her ears from behind. "Just relax, princess. I promise I won't hurt you. If you relax your muscles, pleasure will replace any pain."

Breaking their kiss, Aiden coaxes her to look at him.

"Look at me, baby. Everything is going to be fine."

Drawing her attention away from Max behind her, he slides his fingers between her folds and begins to rub her sensitive bud. Pressing his tongue against the crease of her lips, he slips it through as she opens them slightly.

Aiden's tongue swirls over hers, and for the first time, she can feel every change in texture as it rolls against hers. The light slide of his soft silky underside as it brushes over the top of hers, turning to the bumpy, more aggressive 'give me' side. She can't recall kissing ever being quite so defined before.

Her attention quickly bounces back to Max, pushing his groin forward while subsequently increasing the pressure on his rotating thumb. Within a few minutes, the restrictive band begins to spread, allowing his thumb to pass with ease. Rebecca pulls away from Aiden's mouth and releases a deep moan. His eyes dance across her face, and his lips curl into a smile as he quickly pulls her mouth back to his.

Using his thumb, Max continues to gently stroke her opening while he leans over to offer her some reassuring words. "That's it, princess. The more you relax, the better it'll feel."

When he slowly pulls away, she can feel the sudden void, and her head flings around to search him out. He doesn't leave her searching long. Lifting her onto his lap, he slides her back down on his shaft in one quick motion.

He leans back, pulling her tight against his chest, and allowing Aiden room to glide up behind her. Aiden rests his hand on her lower back and positions himself at her rear entrance. "Just relax, baby."

Noticing her wince slightly at the pressure, Max grabs her face and slides his tongue over hers. His kiss is so demanding she's easily lost to his lips and relaxes once again.

She's so wrapped up in Max's kiss she barely notices Aiden's initial penetration until he lets out a moan and pushes in deeper. She breaks the kiss, and her hand flies back to grab his thigh. "Fuck!"

Aiden stops, and Max takes hold of her nipple, twirling it between his thumb and forefinger, sending exciting little tingles back to her core. Looking almost pained, Aiden grabs her hip and tilts his head to see her face. "Shit. I'm sorry, baby. I'll take my time."

He pulls out slightly then nudges forward a bit further. Rebecca knows he means well, but this action seems to be causing some pain. Unable to relax into his pace, she takes a deep breath and backs herself onto him with a deep moan. Aiden is caught off guard. He inhales sharply, trying to remain perfectly still as he watches himself disappear inside her. "Fuck yeah, baby! That was perfect."

Realizing what has just happened, Max grabs her ass cheeks and pushes upward, alternating thrusts with

Aiden.

Aiden scans her body, absolutely loving the way her flesh flushes with rapture. When her head falls forward, and the sounds escaping her are of pure pleasure. It's not hard to tell she's completely lost to the moment.

Rebecca has never felt anything quite like this before. The multitude of sensations are over the top. It's a true 'I don't give a fuck about anything else but this feeling' type of euphoria. She knows she may face embarrassment later, but right now – she loves every stroke.

Pure fucking Heaven –

She knows she's moaning, she can hear it, but she can't stop. The sensations ripping through her right now own her body and mind. There is no control at this moment. Her body is crying for release. She couldn't stop now even if she wanted to.

With each stroke, waves of exhilarating excitement ripple through her. Her body begins to tremble, and muscles in her stomach tense. Her head crashes against Max's chest. "Holy — Shit! I'm gonna cum!" She cries out without even realizing she's spoken until it's too late.

An inner explosion tightens her muscles into spasm, and it's as if it causes a chain reaction. Both Aiden and Max's grasps seem to get tighter, and their thrusts suddenly pick up speed. Max lets out a roar as he swells inside her, and at the same time, Aiden presses forward with a guttural moan.

With Aiden draped over her back and her head against Max's chest, she can feel the vibrations of their hearts as they thump next to her flesh. The heat from their release has left her feeling thoroughly sated, and when she lifts her head, she opens her eyes to find Max's blues staring back at her. "Hey, princess. How are you feeling?"

Nodding, Rebecca lets out a nervous chuckle of embarrassment. Partly from after sex, 'Oh my god, what did I just do?' humiliation and partly because she's not sure how to answer that question without sounding like a complete nymphomaniac.

Aiden releases himself from her body and slides over beside them so he can see her face. "Are you okay, Rebecca? I mean, I know you're okay, but are you okay with this whole thing?"

She can feel her cheeks heat as she takes a deep breath and nods. "I'll admit, I was worried at first, but it was actually okay. I liked it." She climbs off Max and takes a seat between them. "I'm not sure it's something I'd want to do all the time, but I'm open to a now and again adventure."

Max kisses her cheek. "That's the best news I've heard all day, princess. I'm pretty sure we'd like to do that again."

Aiden pulls her into his lap and smiles. "I'm glad you enjoyed it."

He glances over at Max. "We don't always have to include Max, but you're right. It makes for a nice adventure now and then." Kissing her on her temple, he nudges her off his lap. "What do you say we head over to our room?"

Rebecca nods, suddenly feeling the need to leave. She stands trying to steady herself when Max grabs her arm, pulling her into his lap with a deep kiss. "Goodnight, princess. Thanks for an amazing evening."

Trying to get back to her feet, Aiden takes her hand and helps her toward the steps. Stepping out onto the floor, she smiles back. "Goodnight, Max. The pleasure was mutual."

Throwing on one of Aiden's dress shirts from the back of the door, she holds her finger up. "Just let me pee first."

Smirking, Aiden perches himself by the bathroom door. "Go ahead. I'll wait here."

When Rebecca emerges from the bathroom, Aiden is leaning against the wall in a pair of black shorts waiting patiently. She looks around curiously. "Where's Max?"

He takes her hand and shrugs. "I'm not sure. I think he's getting something to eat. Are you ready to go?"

"Mm-hmm."

She no sooner closes the door to Max's suite when Aiden lets out a roar and picks her up, throwing her over his shoulder. "Haha, let's go to our room so I can ravage you, little missy."

He strides down the path to their suite with Rebecca dangling down his back in a fit of giggles. Kicking the door open, he jogs down the hall to their room and flops her down on the bed. Jumping over to straddle her, he holds her hands above her head and stares down at her like a tiger guarding his prey. "I thought I'd never get you all to myself again."

Rebecca lays at his mercy under his big body while he holds her wrists in one of his hands and slowly undoes the buttons on her shirt. "I thought maybe we could use tonight to explore each other. You know, close in some gaps. I want to know more about you." He looks down into her eyes with a grin. "I mean unless you truly are open for more sex. I'm good with that too."

She looks down at the buttons as he continues to undo her shirt and smirks as she raises her brow. "If we're just talking, why are you taking off my shirt?"

Opening her shirt, he runs his hand between her breasts and kisses her lightly. "Because people tend to bare their souls when their bodies are bare."

He stands to discard his shorts then points to the shirt. "Come on, toss it to the floor."

Rebecca sits forward, sliding the shirt from her shoulders and drops it to the floor. "What exactly do you want to know?"

Grabbing a couple of beers from the mini-fridge at the end of the room, he cracks one open and hands it to her. "I want to know everything. In return, I'll tell you whatever you want to know about me." He kisses her and smiles. "There are no wrong answers, Becca. Just life."

She nods. "Okay. Max said before that your parents were dead to you both. Why?"

Aiden takes a big slug of his beer as his eyes grow wide. "Whoa! Talk about a gutshot right off the bat." A smile stretches across his face, and he reaches out and pats her hand. "Nah, I'm just fucking with you." Rubbing his beard, he focuses on something off in the distance and takes a deep breath. "Well, they were never really parents. They'd come by Nan and Pop's maybe once or twice a week at first. Said they had to work a lot, but they weren't working. They were getting high and gambling." He takes a deep breath, glancing at her, then continues. "Anyway, after a while, they just stopped coming altogether. So, as far as Max and I are concerned – they're dead. It's easier that way." Slugging back on his beer, he looks at her and smiles. "We never talk about them. Nan & Pop raised us. Hey! We'll have to take you to meet Nan and Pop. You'll love them."

Aiden reaches out and shakes her foot playfully with a smile. "So, what about you? Your parents, your family? You must have someone besides Emma."

She nods. "I have my Dad. I next to never speak to him. He works crazy hours on the oil rigs in Alberta. I think the last time I actually saw him was for two days about three years ago. We talk when we can, but it's usually pretty brief."

"Tell me about your millions. How did you two come into your money? Obviously, it's not from an inheritance. Did you win it?"

Aiden chuckles. "We certainly didn't win it," he says, shaking his head. "Would you like the short and to the point answer or a detailed rundown?"

She gives him a big smile. "Oh, I'll definitely take the detailed answer."

He shoves her back on the bed and opens her legs. Climbing between them, he lays his head on her inner thigh and begins to talk. "Well, Nan and Pop didn't have a lot of money, and I knew I'd need a college education to be able to make any real cash. So... When Max and I seen an ad for exotic dancers, we decided to go for it. It would only be until I had enough to pay for tuition, so it wasn't that big of a deal. Besides, the attention of some beautiful ladies wasn't all that unappealing either."

Rebecca laughs and runs her hand through his hair. "I bet it was quite the bonus most nights."

Wiping his hand over his face, he smiles. "Ah, yes. Work perks! That's what we called them." He chuckles. "We had our share of wild nights. We were young, and we had a lot of fun, that's for sure. Anyway, we had been working out, and the ladies seemed to like our looks. We just needed to learn how to dance. One of our friends knew this guy that was a choreographer, and he worked out an amazing routine for us. Everyone loved the fact that we were twins, so we danced together. It drove the ladies wild. They gave us the gig and tagged us Double Trouble." He smirks, patting her leg. "We made a shitload of cash, and I went to college." He takes a deep breath. "When I finished, I found some investors and opened an extremely successful company." He shrugs. "The one you now know as Collins Enterprises. I gave Max 30% of the company because without his help and his investment money, I wouldn't have been able to go through college. I had made my first million dollars by the time I was 24."

Still stroking his hair, Rebecca looks down at him. "That's pretty amazing. I love that you two are so close, and now I also understand how you're both such great dancers."

Aiden laughs, sitting up to grab his beer. "Yeah, I still

really enjoy dancing, especially with you. It's alluring on an intimate level. You're a perfect fit between us, Becca."

Her eyes scan the length of his body while her fingers flit across his chest. "Mmm, you fit nicely too, Mr. Collins."

Before Rebecca even realizes what has happened, Aiden rolls over and crawls on top of her, with a growl. "I'm done talking for tonight. How about you?"

She wraps her arms around him and nips at his bottom lip. "Mm-hmm. Talking can be so overrated sometimes."

"Mmm. It sure can." His hand slides between her thighs, running his fingers through her dampness as he glides down her body. "I've gotta have a taste." Clasping the back of her knees, he pushes them to her chest. His tongue runs between her folds, passed the very ass he had been buried in only a couple of hours ago.

Her hand flies to his head. "Jesus, Aiden. That's still pretty sensitive. If you want to do this, let's just do it. I don't need foreplay right now."

A moan rumbles from his chest, and he looks up into her eyes. "Fuck, you sound so hot when you talk like that."

Wasting no time, he rests back on his haunches and flips her over, pulling her hips toward him. He rubs the head of his dick through her wetness and pushes forward. "Damn, girl, I can't let you go."

So unlike him, but I love it!

Rebecca rocks back against him, meeting each thrust of his hips. "Jesus, that's deep, Aiden." He pulls out slowly, grinding himself back in just as slow. She drops her head forward, her voice deep with arousal. "Holy shit."

Circling her hips as she tries to keep his pace, she can feel her inner muscles contract.

Slapping her ass, he pulls out. "Oh, no. Not yet, princess."

Placing himself at the opening of her ass, he grips her hips and slowly pushes forward until he feels her body accept him. His head drops back as a quick wave of excitement spreads from his groin.

Rebecca inhales sharply, and it takes all his willpower to remain still. He takes a deep breath, trying to rein himself back in. "How are you doing? You okay, baby?"

She nods, reaching back to grab his thigh. "I'm okay. It's not as tender as it was earlier."

Growling against her neck, he slowly pushes forward and reaches between her thighs. "God, you feel so fucking good."

He rolls her swollen bud between his fingers and begins to pump.

She lets out a husky moan, suddenly finding pleasure in each stroke. "Oh! - Shit, Aiden! I think I'm going to cum!"

When she clamps down on his shaft like a pulsating vice, he can't hold back any longer. "Fuck, yes." He grips her hips, thrusting deeper. "Oh – god!"

Holding her in place for one more thrust, he empties himself into her bottom. When he releases her hips, her body gives way beneath him, falling flat to the bed. He pulls her hair back from her face with a chuckle. "You've had an exhausting night, huh? You okay?"

She doesn't move. A mere groan escapes her. "Mm-hmm. I'm fine."

Chuckling, he kisses her shoulder. "Why don't I get you a cloth?"

"Okay." She can't seem to muster any real sentences. Sleep is her only request, and it's creeping up on her quicker then it ever has.

Aiden pulls her tight to his chest, wrapping his body around her. "Goodnight, princess."

"G'night." There is no more energy left in her right now.

~~~

Bright and early the next morning, they wake to Max banging and yelling outside the door. "Hey! You two better get up. We need to head home."

Rebecca quickly springs up only to have Aiden pull her back down. "Fuck that. He can go on his own. We're staying."

"Aiden, you don't even know what it's about. It could be important. Let's at least go see what's going on." She pulls out of his arms and shrugs on a robe as she makes her way to the door. She turns the deadbolt and hollers, "Come in."

Rebecca barely moves out of the way when Max bursts through the door. His face is tight with frustration as he stabs his hand through his hair. "Natasha called. She said Alex Healey called her in a rage. He wants to speak with you." His eyes dart to Aiden behind her. "He claims he has a copy of the contract between Rebecca and me —" He shakes his head. "I mean you."

Okay, wait a minute...

A contract between Rebecca and me? And did he just stab his hand into his hair? Now that I think about it, last night I think I recall Aiden calling me princess — Fuck!!! They did it again!!

Rebecca stands with her hands on her hips. "You two are fucking ridiculous!"

The suspected Aiden sits down on the bed, looking at Rebecca with his brow raised in question while Max moves forward and takes her hand. "I'm serious, Rebecca. He wants to see you by tomorrow at noon, or he's turning the contract over to the press."

She picks up the throw pillows from the lounger and starts tossing them at the brothers. "You two are assholes! You swapped places with each other last night! I fucking knew it!!"

Shoving passed the real Aiden, she heads to the bathroom and slams the door.

She can hear Max laughing from the other side of the room while Aiden bangs on the door. "Come on, Rebecca. Let me in. We won't do it again without your knowledge. I swear."

Turning on the shower, she calls out, "You know what? Just book me on a flight back this afternoon. I'll go deal with Alex myself. The contract he has isn't signed by me. I only signed it electronically on your phone."

Max exhales exaggeratedly. "She's right, bro. Have our lawyers say it's something he made up as a disgruntled ex-boyfriend."

Aiden looks at Max. "That's fine and good, but my signature is on it, along with my cell number. Oh, and did I mention Natasha said he's also threatening to press charges on you for assault and battery? He apparently has witnesses of you smashing his head into my car. Natasha's already calling our lawyers, but we still need to get back. Rebecca shouldn't have to deal with this dick on her own."

Max stabs his legs into a pair of track pants and looks at Aiden. "Oh, she won't. We'll go."

Walking out of the bathroom in her robe with a towel wrapped around her head, she looks at them. "I'm really sorry about the trouble Alex is causing. We haven't been together in a long time, so I'm not really sure why he's pulling this now." She waves her finger between Aiden and Max with a perturbed gaze. "Just because I feel a little responsible for the trouble, don't think I have forgotten about you two swapping places last night. I'm still mad about that."

Swatting her bottom, Max leans down and kisses her cheek. "Yeah, but you have to admit, last night was pretty fucking amazing, Becca."

Pulling a brief smile from her, she nods. "That doesn't make it okay."

Aiden wraps his arms around her and kisses her forehead then leans back, giving her a big smile. "You're right, we were wrong, and we're sorry. As for this Alex thing, we'll fix it together. Don't worry."

She shakes her head. "I left the contract in my desk at home. I knew I should never have trusted either of them.

This is my fault."

Max cups her chin and lifts her head to face him. "Becca, this guy and your sleazy friend need to be taught a lesson. This is not your fault. Aiden is right. We'll go back and deal with this together." He scans her face. "Hey! We should marry you and Aiden here first. Then that contract truly is nothing more than an engagement arrangement." He jumps on the bed with a grin. "Shit. Get our lawyer on the phone, bro! I bet that'll work!"

Aiden pulls out his phone and dials their lawyer handing the phone to Max. "I hope you know what you're talking about." He looks at Rebecca. "Are you even willing to marry me?"

Rebecca looks at him, stunned. "Uh, you mean like a real marriage?"

Smiling, Aiden throws his arms around her. "Yeah. Like a real marriage. We can get married here this afternoon then fly out this evening. When Alex sees you tomorrow, you'll be Mrs. Aiden Collins, and that contract will mean absolutely nothing," he says with a grin.

She stares up at him with wide eyes. "Wow, Aiden. That's a bit drastic. Don't you think? Can't we just go back and let your lawyer handle this? Marriage is forever in my world. I need some time to think about something as serious as this." She slowly sinks onto the bed as though her body is a deflating balloon and puts her head in her hands.

This guy is just full of surprises.

This is it. This must be where I get punked! It took a while, but I knew it was coming.

Max hands Aiden the phone. "Here, bro. You need to send him a copy of the contract, but he's convinced it'll deflect any nonsense Alex may try to cause with the press."

Grabbing the phone from Max, he sends a copy of the contract to their lawyer and within minutes, the phone rings. He answers it, walking out of the room to take the call.

Taking Rebecca's hands, Max looks into her eyes. "Listen, fuck the press. They make shit up all the time. Besides, it'll only be popular until the next big story next week. Trust me, Aiden can handle this, princess." He gives her a serious look. "The real question is... are you sure you're ready to get married today?"

She searches his eyes for the answer, but it's not there. "I-I'm not sure."

Max pulls her to his chest and kisses the top of her head. "It's okay. Don't do anything you're not ready to do. It was just an idea, maybe a stupid one. I kind of thought you two were already talking about marriage, that's all."

Shaking her head, she smiles, suddenly unsure of herself.

"It's just… I don't know what this is exactly. I mean, I really love you guys. You two could grow on someone very quickly, and you have." A nervous laugh escapes her as she watches Aiden enter the room with a huge grin. She quickly reaches into the open safe and grabs her passport stuffing it into her purse.

"Max, you're fucking brilliant! It'll absolutely work." He stands in front of Rebecca and takes her hands. "Well, what do you think, Baby? What do you say we just do this? Let's turn this adventure into forever." His smile is so bright the corners of his mouth nearly reach his eyes.

Stepping back with shaky knees, Rebecca looks at him, unsure of what to say. "I-I'm - Aiden, I'm gonna go grab my things from Max's room and try to digest all this. I just need some processing time."

Max and Aiden give each other a quick glance as Rebecca turns to leave. "Of course, just don't be too long. We need to book the officiant for this afternoon, and I'm sure you'll want a dress."

Glancing back, she smiles, giving him a quick nod. "Right. I won't be too long. I just need to let this all sink in." She stops as she reaches the door and turns back to face him. "Aiden, I truly do love you."

Smiling, he blows her a kiss. "I love you too, Rebecca."

Aiden stabs his hand through his hair and looks down at his watch for the 20th time as he paces by the window. "It's been almost two hours, Max. I'm going to go get her."

Standing abruptly, Max wastes no time following behind him. "I'm coming with you. She's in my room."

When they arrive at Max's room, it's empty. They call out for her, but there is no sign of Rebecca anywhere. Aiden flops down on the sofa running his hands through his hair. "Fuck! She wouldn't have gone back to Victoria alone. Would she?"

Max steps out of his bedroom with a note in his hand and gives it to Aiden. "I'm sorry, bro. It looks like she left."

Looking up at Max, his face drops as he takes the note from his hands.

Dear Aiden,

I'm sorry. I'm not sure I'm ready to commit to forever yet. I will take care of Alex. You don't have to worry about that. I'll tell the media and anyone else that asks we were dating. Hell, I believed we were anyway. I'll let them know we had a fight here in Jamaica when I told you about a phony contract I had drawn up to give to you as a joke.

Please don't misunderstand my leaving. I think you two

are great, but forever is a really long time. I hope you can find it in your heart to forgive me.

Rebecca xo

Tossing the note to the floor, he glares back up at Max. "God Damn it! Call Andre and get the fucking plane ready!"

Chapter 11 – Oh, Hell No!

Marriage? Oh, hell, no!

After telling the guys that she needs some time to digest this morning's events before she can make a decision, Rebecca grabs her passport and wallet from the closet safe by the bathroom and scurries off down the hall to Max's suite. No, she doesn't need time to make a decision. Her mind is already made up. She has no intention of marrying anyone today. The only thing she'll be doing today is grabbing the next flight out of Jamaica.

Wearing only flip flops, a bikini top and a pair of shorts, she throws on one of Max's shirts and leaves a note for Aiden on the dresser in Max's room. There is no way she's about to make a life long commitment over a 30-day contract.

The next flight to Victoria has a brief stopover in Toronto, and it doesn't leave for another three hours, but it's her only option. Surely if she waits in Max's room, they'll come looking for her before then. So, she grabs her purse and takes a taxi to the airport.

Her nerves are exploding. She knows she should have said a proper goodbye to Aiden and Max, but there is no way they would have let her leave without them. If she knows anything about the Collins brothers, she knows they won't be far behind her. Her biggest dilemma at this moment is the fact that she's booked on a 10-hour commercial flight home that doesn't leave for another 3 hours. Will she be able to beat them back?

After witnessing the way Max handled Alex that day at the Purple Lion, and now hearing Alex wants to press charges against him for trying to protect her, it's best if she goes alone. Rebecca has already decided on what she will be telling Alex. Sure, it might be a lie, but he's lied to her many times. There's no reason she should feel guilty lying to him about something that's none of his damn business.

When Rebecca arrives at the Sangster International Airport, she checks in and passes through security. She wants to be out of direct view should Aiden and Max decide to take a chance coming to check for her. There's still a fair bit of time to spare before her flight leaves, so she makes herself comfortable in a booth near the back in Air Margaritaville.

She's sipping on her margarita when finally, after what feels like an eternity, they call her flight.

'Now boarding flight 1804 to Toronto on Air Canada

Rouge. All passengers, please make your way to gate 19.'

With a breath of relief, she grabs her purse and heads for the gate. Handing over her identification, the flight attendant points her through the gate. It's just over four hours to get into Toronto, but at least there is no juggling of planes. While they sit waiting for new passengers to board, Rebecca takes a minute and checks her phone. She has messages from both Aiden and Max.

Aiden –

Rebecca, I'm not angry. Please do not meet up with Alex on your own. Wait for us at my house. The entry code is the day we met 9202017.

The thought of him changing his entry code to the day they met brings a smile to her face and reinforces the fact that she needs to deal with this on her own. There is no way she can allow Alex to tarnish Aiden's reputation. It's her fault she left the contract at her place to begin with.

She swipes Aiden's message closed and opens the next one from Max.

Princess, text me when you land. We just need to know you're safe. If you are meeting up with Alex, please promise you'll stay in a public place.

Rebecca starts to type out a response to Max, letting him know she's okay, then stops and turns off her phone. It's been almost eight hours since she left them in her and Aiden's room. For all she knows, they could be just about to Victoria themselves by now, and she still has another four and a half hour flight ahead of her before she'll get there. To send a response to Max now, they'll surely be waiting for her at the airport instead of checking Aiden's and her place first. She needs that extra time to try and convince Alex to give her back the contract.

As expected, she can't seem to sleep a wink on the remaining flight from Toronto to Victoria. Her mind continually keeps sliding to thoughts of Aiden and Max. She knows they've got to be in Victoria by now.

What will she say to Aiden when she sees him again? Is sorry really going to be enough to mend their budding relationship considering the way she left? Sure, he dissolved their contract, but deep down, she feels as if she owes him something better then disappearing without a goodbye. And Max. He went out of his way to plan the trip to Jamaica to keep Alex away from her.

Her mind has been racing the entire flight, and her body is tight with tension as the pilot activates the seatbelt sign and announces their descent. She's not typically a nail biter, but she's chewed her thumbnail down so badly she can taste blood.

Maybe she should have just married Aiden. On the one hand, it makes no sense to be running away from the man who has been nothing but kind and understanding to run back to deal with a loser that has treated her like she was merely there for his convenience since they were teenagers. However, on the other hand, if she doesn't deal with Alex, she knows all too well he will do anything he can to try and destroy Aiden, and they would always have him meddling in their lives.

When Rebecca's flight lands, she pulls out her phone and calls Alex. Hearing his voice on the other end, she instantly wants to hang up.

'Hello'

"Hey, Alex. It's Becca."

Strangely enough, the asshole almost sounds shocked to hear from her. As if he wasn't the one who demanded that she come back or he'd send a copy of that stupid contract between her and Aiden to the press.

'Wow! Hey, Becca. Where are you?'

Rolling her eyes at his exaggerated tone, she grabs the strap of her purse and fastens it over her shoulder as she heads down the aisle to exit the plane. "Where the hell do you think I am, Alex? I just landed in Victoria. I'm just walking off the plane."

Rebecca can hear him release a breath of relief as his tone softens.

'Are you alone?'

She doesn't even try to disguise her annoyance as the words rush into the phone. "Christ, Alex! Of course, I'm alone! I believe you have something that belongs to me, and I'm here to get it back. Now, stop with the damn games. I don't have time for this nonsense."

His breathing increases, and she can hear gravel crunching. She can literally picture him jogging down his driveway as he speaks to her.

'Give me ten minutes, and I'll pick you up in front of arrivals. I'm already in my truck.'

Just as she thought, Rebecca hears the door shut and his truck starts, but before she can hang up the phone, Alex calls out to her.

'Hey, Becca.'

"What, Alex?"

'I still love you.'

With little interest in entertaining his remark, Rebecca disconnects the call and makes her way through the airport to wait for him out front of arrivals. Her phone instantly begins to vibrate as she watches the screen light up with messages from Aiden and Max.

Aiden —

'Rebecca, we're back in Victoria. We've been to both my house and yours. Where are you? Baby, I swear I'm not upset with you, but I am worried. Please, let me know you're okay.

A stab of guilt grabs her, and she can feel her heart sink as she reads Aiden's message. She really does owe it to him to let him know she's arrived and is safe. She sends him back a quick text.

"Aiden, I'm fine. Please don't worry."

Max —

'Princess, just text me when you land. I promise we're not mad. We just need to know you're safe.'

'Hey, Max. I'm sorry for the way I left, but I'm not sure I'm ready for the whole marriage thing. Anyway, I just wanted to let you know I'm back in Victoria, and I'm safe. Alex is on his way to pick me up from the airport. Please don't worry. I'll be sure we stay in a public place.'

As she slips her phone back into her pocket, Alex's big blue 4x4 pulls around the corner, and her heart immediately starts to race. Damn, she can't believe she agreed to meet up with him.

The truck screeches to a halt alongside her, and the driver's door springs open. She freezes when he rushes to her side with a wide smile. His arms wrap around her, and he places a kiss on her forehead. "God, I'm so glad you're back. I've missed you so much."

She briefly recalls when his arms were a comfort, and when his kiss made her weak, but those days are long gone.

Now his kiss makes her feel queasy, and she can't seem to break free of his arms quick enough.

"Alex, stop! This isn't a social call. I came so you wouldn't try to ruin a good man's life over bullshit. That contract was supposed to be a personal joke between Aiden and me. I drew it up on his computer from one of his templates. It was never meant for anyone's eyes but ours."

Breaking free of his grasp, she glares up at him. "And you had no business being in my fucking house."

Shocked by her reaction, Alex lowers his eyes to hers with a crooked smile. "You seem to forget that Emma and I are friends. I went by to see her."

He tries to take her hand to help her into his truck, but she pulls away. "Don't touch me. I can get in myself."

Throwing his hands up defensively with a smirk, Alex backs away. "Okay, listen. Let's just go someplace so we can talk privately. I'm sure you must be hungry after your flight. Is Fish on Fifth still one of your favourites?"

Rebecca is so nervous. She ignores his question and settles into the passenger seat as he shuts the door. Barely able to steady her hands, she latches her seatbelt and watches him walk around the front of the truck. Taking a few deep breaths, she clasps her hands in her lap to stop them from trembling.

God, have I ever felt this nervous around him before?

When he jumps into the truck, he leans forward, resting his arm over the steering wheel and looks over at her. "Why are you so damn nervous?"

Flitting his finger back and forth between them. "This is just you and me. We're just gonna go for dinner and talk. Surely you're not afraid to be alone with me, are you?"

Studying her composure, he shakes his head as the corner of his mouth pulls into a slight smile. "You really need to calm down. The last thing I would do is hurt you."

He flops back against his seat and glances back over at her. "Now, you never did confirm. Is Fish on Fifth, okay?

Staring out the front window, she nods. There is only one thing on her mind – get the contract back, but Fish on Fifth will keep them in public. "Sure, I guess I could use something to eat."

On their way into Sidney, Alex keeps glancing in her direction. She knows he's dying to spark up a conversation, but she's not about to initiate one. Finally, he can't refrain any longer. "So, how was Jamaica? Did you have a good time?"

God, she wants to smack him in the mouth. He knows damn well she had to cut her vacation short to deal with his childish nonsense. "It was great until we were ignorantly disturbed with false accusations of Aiden making an indecent proposal."

"False accusations?!"

Alex's voice is stern as he glances at her with his brow raised. "Come on. Let's not play games, Bec. This is me you're talking to, and don't forget I have a copy of that contract."

"How many times do I have to tell you? It's not a real contract! You have a fucking prank that I typed up for my boyfriend!"

She slaps her hands against the seat in frustration. She'd love nothing more than to lunge at him right now. "Look, Alex. The first time Aiden set eyes on that document was when he received the copy you sent Natasha. I hadn't even had a chance to give it to him yet!"

Parking out front of the restaurant, he turns to face her,

tipping his head at her in question. "Really, Becca? Is that so? Then tell me something. How did his signature get on the contract, and why is his cell number written on the top?"

Attempting to look calm, she shrugs slightly. "Like I said, it was a template for Natasha, so Aiden doesn't have to be there for every document. I added his cell number for authenticity."

He throws his head back with laughter. "Authenticity? Oh, that's a good one."

She looks at him curiously. "Wait, how did you know it was Aiden's cell number written on the top?"

Pulling his keys from the ignition, he shrugs with a smirk. "How else? I phoned it."

Alex jumps out of the truck and meets her at her door just as her feet hit the sidewalk. "I would have helped you down."

Ducking under his arm with little attitude spared, she strides toward the restaurant. "Thanks, but I don't need your help."

He stands back with his hands on his hips, watching as she yanks the door open with an exaggerated huff. "Wow. I'm not sure I've ever seen this side of you before."

Without so much as glancing back, she shrugs. "Well, if you give me back the damn document, you won't need to see me ever again, Alex. That is the only reason I just took a 10-hour flight back here."

She sits down at a table against the window and tries to focus on an older woman reading at the bus stop outside to avoid making eye contact with him. "I mean, at this point, I'm considering having you charged with break and enter as well as theft of my personal property."

From the expression on his face, it looks like she's finally gotten his attention until he leans forward and licks his lips. "Come closer. There's something else I need to tell you."

Leaning forward cautiously, she can feel goosebumps erupt across the surface of her skin as his lips brush against her ear. "I did take a pair of your panties," he says, leaning back with a condescending smile. She had forgotten how quick his reflexes were as his hand snaps up to grab her wrist, a mere second before she can connect with his face.

"Whoa. Relax. Emma let me in. I didn't break into anything except your laundry hamper." He releases her wrist with a chuckle. "Are you really going to try and have your boyfriend charged with keeping a pair of your panties? Because I'm pretty sure that's not going to stand up in court."

"You're not my fucking boyfriend!"

He shrugs. "You're right! I'm supposed to be your god damn fiancé."

"I am not discussing that nonsense with you right now. I have a boyfriend. His name is Aiden. What I want to know is, if you didn't break into my room, how did you get the document?"

Shaking his head, he gives her a cynical smile. "Come on, Becca. Call it what it is for Christ's sake. It's a god damn contract between you and Aiden Collins for sexual services in exchange for money. It's not a pretend document. And for your information, the contract was sitting on your kitchen counter when I went over to see Emma. She said she found it in your desk drawer when she was searching for a pair of scissors."

Folding her arms across her chest, she instantly feels the anger rush through her.

Emma needs a damn throat punch. She was snooping, simple as that.

"So the pair of you are nothing more than snoops, thieves, and liars. Like I already told Em, you two deserve one another."

His brows draw together, and his face reddens. "I have never wanted Emma!"

"You wanted her just fine that day I brought my new car by the Purple Lion. You know, the day you had your tongue lodged down her throat," she shoots back a little harsher than intended.

Enjoying the sight of his obvious unease, her eyes survey the flush of his face as he chews on the inside of his cheek. Apparently, he was unaware that she knew about that little incident.

Score one for Becca!

Not ready to let it go, she continues. "Oh, yes. I know all about that little indiscretion between you and Emma. Not that it matters now. Emma was only the icing on the cake. I've watched you parade around with several women publicly over the past year, don't forget. I'm numb to it all now." She waves her hand through the air as if brushing it off like yesterday's news. "I knew the moment you left. We were never getting married. It might have hurt for the first few months, but that feeling has long since passed. Now, I feel nothing for you."

Alex reaches for her hand, and for the first time, she can see regret in his eyes. She reminds herself, 'Too little too late' and pulls her hands back, placing them in her lap.

"Don't touch me, Alex. Just don't."

Acknowledging her reaction with a humorous smirk, he waves to the waitress for the check. "Fine. Why don't we go for a walk? We can talk out on the pier while we get some air. You've always loved it out there."

"I really just want the document back. I think it's evident there's nothing left between us. I mean, Christ, you cheated on me before you even left. I need someone I can trust. That's not you."

The waitress drops the check on the table and stands with her hand on her hip, staring at Alex. Instantly, Rebecca can feel her cheeks start to burn.

Oh, this is just great! Another one of his conquests, I presume.

He looks up at the waitress with a sour face. "Thanks. I'll bring it up to the register. Now, if you don't mind, we're talking."

Bending over, the waitress slaps her palms down on the table and glares at Rebecca then turns her stare back to Alex. "I thought you said you were done with her. Why haven't you returned my calls?"

Rebecca rolls her eyes at Alex.

Yep. Seen that coming a mile away.

His face drops as his eyes focus in on her, and the realization hits him.

Ahh, shit! Perfect timing. It's that chick from the night before I left town. What's her name again?

Squinting up at her, he snaps his fingers and points. "Bethany, right?"

She purses her lips and raises her brows. The annoyance is evident in her tone as she stands, placing her hand on her hip. "Pfft! It's Brittany."

"Right. Well, Brittany, as you can see. Things have changed." He shrugs, giving her a lopsided smile, then turns his attention back to Rebecca.

A very unimpressed Brittany kicks his chair and walks away in a tiff. Rebecca holds her hand out toward the pissed off waitress and raises her brow. "There you go. I rest my case."

Frustrated, he exhales slowly, tossing a fifty on the table and holds his hand out to her. "Come on. Let's take a walk along the pier so we can talk."

Ignoring his outstretched hand, Rebecca gets up and walks toward the door. Once she reaches the sidewalk, she swears she catches a glimpse of Max's hummer, but when she looks back, it's gone.

It's getting late, and she's completely done with the pleasantries. If Max and Aiden are in the area, she needs to get that contract back and get away from Alex. A scowl forms on her face as she stares at him. "Come on, Alex. Where's the god damn contract? I just want it back. After all, that is why I'm here, isn't it?"

He purses his lips and nods. "Actually, I wanted to talk to you, but if that's what it'll take for you to loosen up so we can talk. Just give me a minute, and I'll grab it."

Taking off toward the truck, he returns with a manilla folder stuffed under his arm. "Okay? Now can we go for a walk? You can have it once we get out on the pier."

Alex turns and starts walking, glancing back only briefly to wave his hand at her to follow.

"Ugh!"

She strides up beside him, and they walk in silence along Bevan Avenue toward the pier. The moment they step onto the first wooden plank, Rebecca can't help herself. She holds out her hand. "Okay, we're here. Now, let me see the document."

His eyes spring open wide, and he hands her the folder. "Wow, Bec. With that attitude, there's no way it's just a gag. It's a valid contract, just like I said."

Snatching the folder from his hands, she opens it to find it empty. Her face begins to burn as she glares up at him and slams the folder against his chest. "Alex, stop screwing around! Where is it?"

Laughing, he grabs her arm to keep her from leaving and looks down at her. "I'm not that stupid. Once I hand it over, you'll leave, and I'm not done talking yet."

Her voice drips with venom as she struggles to break free of his grasp. "Then say what you have to say. I've had a long flight, and I'm too tired for these games."

Sliding his hand down her arm, he wraps his hand around her wrist and gently tugs her forward. "Walk with me."

Not wanting to make a scene, she follows alongside him and listens as he talks. "You see, Becca. Men have stronger urges than women, and you never quite understood that, did you? I tried so hard to be faithful, but you just wouldn't give in, and the chicks – god, the chicks were throwing themselves at me like you can't imagine. What was I supposed to do?"

Glancing down at her, he tries to gauge her response, but her gaze doesn't waver from the ocean ahead. "Obviously, you haven't been saving yourself for me. I mean, there's no way that you can tell me you haven't been fucking Collins, can you?" Tugging back on her hand, he stops to look into her eyes. "Well, can you?"

Trying to free her hand, he squeezes it tighter. "It's none of your damn business who I fuck!"

With a quick snap, he pulls her body tight against his chest, brushing the hair from her face as he speaks through clenched teeth. "Now see, Bec, that's where you're mistaken. You are very much my business. In case you've forgotten, we promised each other forever, remember?"

Taking her hand, he examines her fingers then releases it angrily. "Why the fuck aren't you wearing my ring?"

"Oh, don't look so surprised. I haven't worn it since you left. You never called except for a handful of times, and you only text me the first month you were gone. Why would I wear your ring?"

She walks further along the pier to put a little distance between them and kicks a stray stone off into the water. Leaning against the railing, she looks out across the ocean. "I never said I'd wait for you, and you sure the fuck didn't wait for me."

Grasping at straws, he tries to draw her attention back to the good times they once shared. His voice softens as he stands next to her and holds his hand out toward one of the fishing balconies. "Hey, remember that balcony over there? We used to come out here to make out. In fact, I'll bet our names are still carved in that bench."

Glancing at her, he waves his hand at the small loading dock and chuckles. "And there — remember when we went skinny dipping that night?"

He ducks down to look into her eyes with that seductive smile. The same one she's sure must have broken hundreds of hearts over the past year. "Remember? That's the night I took your virginity. We were right there under the pier. Come on, Becca. Doesn't that mean anything to you?"

Shaking her head, she turns to look back out across the ocean. "No, Alex. It doesn't mean anything to me anymore. Those days are so far removed from my present. In fact, I barely recall any of my time with you. In all honesty, that all feels like it was a lifetime ago."

Stepping up behind her, he grabs hold of the railing, caging her between his arms and presses his groin tight against her bottom. Leaning his head against hers, he nuzzles his nose into her hair and whispers. "Well then, maybe we just need to make some new memories."

As his lips brush her neck, she jerks her head away. "Christ, Alex. Just stop!"

He exhales a heavy breath of frustration as he rests his chin on her shoulder. "Look, I get it. I screwed up. Just tell me what it will take to bring you back to me."

"I'm not coming back to you. That's not why I'm here."

"I personally never thought you were one for money, but shit, if that's what it takes these days. Then name your price. Tell me, how much will it cost me to steal you back from Collins?"

Rebecca can feel the heat flood her body as she tries to spin out from his arms, but Alex grabs hold of her hands. He folds them into a hug across her stomach and presses his body tight against hers. Inhaling deeply against her neck, he moans. "Mmm. God, you smell so fucking good."

Attempting to twist out of his arms, he tightens his grip and lets out a sinister chuckle next to her ear. "Damn, you've gotten feisty. Just relax. I'm not judging you. I'm asking you a serious question. How much will it cost me to get you back?"

He rubs his erection along her bottom. "Mmm. My god, baby. I've missed the feel of you against me."

Struggling to break free of his grasp, her words come out in a deep growl. "Let me fucking go! No amount of money could ever bring me back to a cheater like you."

"Oh, come on. We aren't kids anymore. I know Collins has money. He bought you an expensive car — he has a big house — takes you on expensive vacations. I get it. I can play that game too. I have money now, so just tell me. What is it that will make you happy again? Will a nice house and a half a million bring you back to me for good?"

He spins her around to face him, making sure to keep a firm grip on her hands. "What the fuck is wrong with you? This isn't about money. The problem is you. You can't keep your dick in your pants!"

As he glances down to size up his crotch with a cocky smirk, she brings her knee up, connecting a solid crack to his groin and sends him to his knees. "What the fuck, Becca?! Why do you always have to be such a fucking bitch?!"

Finally free of his grasp, Rebecca darts for the walkway at the end of the pier. "Fuck you, Alex!"

As she shouts back over her shoulder, she collides full force with a solid body. Two big arms wrap around her, and that familiar intoxicating smell of citrus spice wafts a sense of security straight to her nose. Gasping to catch her breath, she lifts her head to look into Aiden's welcoming eyes.

He gently brushes the hair from her face and smiles down at her. "You're okay, baby. I got you."

Tears of relief flood her eyes as she lets go of her fear and melts against his chest. "God, Aiden. I'm so sorry. I thought I could get the contract back, but he wouldn't give it to me. I told him I made it up as a gag, but I don't think he believes it."

Cupping her face in his hands, he wipes her tears away with his thumbs and smiles. "Shh, don't worry about it. It's going to be fine."

Kissing her lightly on the cheek, he protectively tucks

her into his side. "Let's just go home."

As she turns to look back, he faces her forward and starts back down the pier. "Wait. Is that Max?"

She tries to see around him, but he pulls her tighter into his side. "Don't worry about Max. He'll meet us at the car."

Never missing a step, he continues walking them off the pier. As they step onto the walkway and out of view, he squeezes her arm to get her attention. "You know we have no contract between us any longer, right? If you want to leave, you don't have to run. You can come to me and tell me you're leaving. There is no penalty or repercussions. You do understand that, don't you?"

She starts to say something, but he puts his hand out to stop her. "Wait. Let me finish." Leaning her against Max's truck, he takes her hands. "I came here not because I thought you were running from me, but because I think you were trying to protect me from the publicity. Make no mistake. A publicity blooper is never anything I care to experience. Still, it will never rate above your safety."

Placing his hand under her chin, he lifts her face to his. "I worry about you, Rebecca. I'm sure you must know that by now."

"I don't want people to know how we began, and I'm sure you don't either. It's like our dirty little secret that I'd like to keep buried. I told you from the start I didn't need a contract, but you wanted to be able to walk away after 30 days guilt-free if it wasn't what you wanted. Contract or no contract, I would have at least taken the chance." She fixes her eyes on his. "Believe it or not, I might actually love you, Aiden."

Aiden's face is riddled with guilt as he forces a smile. "Yet, the marriage proposal scared you away."

Chuckling nervously, she shrugs. "It was for all the wrong reasons. Besides, This is still really new. I'm not convinced we're ready for marriage. Are you?"

"I'm a decision-maker, Rebecca. I make my mind up on things very quickly. Some people say, 'If you snooze, you lose.' Well, I have to agree. Marriage has never crossed my mind before, and yet, I would without question, marry you tomorrow." Kissing her lightly, he looks into her eyes. "I know I love you."

Ugh! Please don't propose again.

Avoiding the marriage conversation, she decides to change the topic. "What do we do about the contract? You know Alex will likely take it to the press now."

"I doubt he will, but if he does, I'll say you drew it up on one of my templates for fun." He shrugs. "That's what you already told him, right? Let them say what they want. The more I think about it, the less I care. The only thing I care about is that you're safe."

Max's dark shadow jogs toward the truck, and as he comes into full view, all they hear is his big rumbling voice. "Damn, Princess! We missed you."

He holds his arms out to her. "Well, come and give me a hug, damn it. We just flew 9 hours to come and get you."

Laughing, she jumps into his arms and wraps herself around him. "You couldn't have missed me that much. It hasn't even been a full 24 hrs yet."

Sliding down, she pats his chest and gives him a curious gaze. "Now, stop trying to distract me. What did you do to Alex? I saw you heading for him when Aiden pulled me away."

Max shrugs as he opens her door. "I have no idea where he went. He must have left before I got there."

Nodding with a smile, she gives him a playful punch in the arm. "Somehow, I highly doubt that Maxwell."

"Oh, I see. It's Maxwell now, is it?" He darts for her, but Aiden steps between them and halts their every action with one word.

"Enough!"

Sticking her tongue out at Max, she laughs as she climbs

into the passenger seat. "How'd you two know we'd be down at the pier anyway?"

Aiden stands, leaning on her door with a smile. "Because I listen to you. You told me this was your place," he says, using his fingers as quotations. "Where else would he take you?"

Starting the truck, Max glances back at Aiden. "Are we ready to go home?"

His gaze rakes across Becca. "We could always go have a couple of drinks at the Purple Lion and get it all out of our systems in one night. Emma should be working tonight, right?"

Aiden shakes his head. "No, I think we've had enough excitement for tonight. Why don't we go soak in the hot tub? We can have a few drinks and relax."

"Yeah, that sounds good too, as long as I can stay the night. Although, we still have a week's worth of accommodations in Jamaica if you want to head back there."

"You know my house is your house. On the other hand, I'm open to returning to Jamaica if Rebecca wants to go."

Swinging his gaze back to meet hers, he gives her a sly smile. "However, I must remind you that my house offers clothing-optional accommodations with absolutely no restrictions on a 24/7 basis."

"Then I guess there's no need to go back to Jamaica. I'll admit it was a nice getaway, but it's over now," she says, smiling over at him with a shrug.

Laying his hand over hers, he runs his thumb along the top of her hand in a soothing motion. "Maybe we should stop by your place so you can grab some of your things."

She shoots him a worried glance. "Aiden—"

He raises his hand with a slight smile. "I'm not saying we have to get married. I'm simply saying you can stay with me until you find a new place. I have plenty of room, and you can stay as long as you like. There'll be no expenses, so you won't have to worry about work for now."

Max glances back at him and smirks. "I'd take him up on his offer, princess. That sounds like a pretty sweet deal. I personally wouldn't go to work for the prick, but as for grabbing your stuff and staying with him, I'd say that's a solid choice. You know Alex will be back at your house to see Emma." He runs his hand across his beard in contemplation. "You can correct me if I'm wrong, but from that knee you delivered to his groin, it kind of looked as if you don't care to deal with him anymore. Am I right?"

Laughing, she slaps the back of his seat. "Wow, you saw that? I never saw you on the pier until after I ran into Aiden."

"Oh, I saw the whole thing. I wouldn't want to meet your knee, that's for sure. For a little one, you pack quite the force behind those little legs."

"I honestly doubt you would ever give me a reason to do something like that to you, Max."

Aiden rubs her shoulder. "So what do you say? Do we go pick up your stuff? It's completely up to you. We don't have to go tonight. We can always go another time. I just thought it may be easier for you since you said Emma's working right now."

It's not a difficult decision. Aiden's right, with Emma working, the timing is perfect. "Yeah, you're right. Let's go grab it while she's at work. The less I have to deal with them, the better."

Smiles broaden across both brothers' faces. "Great! I can stop by my place and grab a trailer," Max says with a wide grin.

"I appreciate that, Max, but there's no need for a trailer. I'm not taking any of my furniture, just my clothes and my computer." Feeling his eyes on her, Rebecca looks back at Aiden. "Unless, of course, sharing your bed is no longer an option."

A smile slides across Aiden's face. "Baby, I wouldn't have it any other way."

Thanks for Reading

Want to read more?

Check out Contracted to Mr. Collins 2: COMMITMENT

I'd love to hear from you!

Did you enjoy the book? — Word of mouth recommendations travel fast. Please be sure to tell other readers about it.

Did you leave a review? — There's nothing an author appreciates more than an honest review.

Book 1 Contracted to Mr. Collins

Book 2 Contracted to Mr. Collins 2: COMMITMENT

Visit my website:

https://sjturnerstories.com

Follow Me on Twitter

https://www.twitter.com/SJTurner_Author

A proud member of the Independent Author Network

https://www.independentauthornetwork.com/sj-turner.html

About The Author

Sj. Turner

SJ. Turner developed her love for reading at an early age. Stealing her mother's romance novels and tucking them away to read late at night was a common occurrence. The first novel that truly made an impact on her, however, was To Kill a Mockingbird by Harper Lee. It was a story that had stuck with her for many years.

After losing her mother at a young age, poetry became a very big part of SJ's life. As a teen, she used it as a source of expression, a way to release deep emotions. A few of her poems have been published in a poetry library that was released in 2002.

After complaining to a family member about boredom, she was advised to write a book. Within a few months Contracted to Mr. Collins was written. Mainly to amuse family and friends at first, but when the unedited version was uploaded to a self-publishing site, It began to sell. A second book soon followed and the decision was made to pull the books and rework them for a real audience.

Today her novels can be purchased from most major on-line retailers.

The Collins Brothers Series

Contracted To Mr. Collins

Rebecca D'Angelo had heard about the account executive position at Collins Enterprises a few days earlier. With a whopping $75,000 base salary on the line, she was eager to apply. Aspirations soaring, she put together a stunning portfolio and an impressive résumé, then marched herself directly downtown.

With zing in her step, she walked up to the building and read the notice on the front door:
DEADLINE - Résumés for Account Executive position must be received no later than 10 am this morning.
She checked the time on her phone - 9:51 am. Unsure of her exact destination, she began to panic. She darted toward the information desk. At first, Rebecca had no idea what she even ran into – a brick wall?
Crashing to the floor, her latte and portfolio launched into the air. Her momentary thought was, thankfully she had protected her documents with a plastic case. However, that thought abruptly ended when a set of large hands wrapped around her arms and a deep rumbling voice echoed above her. "Jesus Christ! This is not a schoolyard, young lady!"

Looking up, she couldn't believe her eyes. His dark hair was combed back neatly on the top and trimmed into a flawlessly tapered fade on the sides to meet his designer stubbled beard. The most amazing electric blue eyes she had ever seen stood out like stars against a perfect bronze tan, and she could feel the power radiate off his 6' 4" GQ cover body as she watched him wipe her latte from his crisp white dress shirt and expensive Armani suit. There was no mistaking who this man was — Aiden Collins, CEO of Collins Enterprises.

Her only thought... 'Shit!'

Amazingly, she's made it to the final round of interviews, but today's interview will be conducted by none other than — Aiden Collins himself. Yep. That's right. That means her fate at Collins Enterprises now lies solely in his hands.
On the bright side, it's been three weeks since the latte accident, and she has made it this far. That must mean he's forgotten. Right?

This book is rated 18+ Due to Adult situations and Language

Contracted To Mr. Collins 2: Commitment

Within only a few short hours of being back in Victoria, Rebecca has had some eye-opening truths thrown her way. Suddenly, who does and who doesn't have her best interest in mind becomes very clear. One thing is for certain, her 'best friend' Emma has never been someone she could trust.

Maybe a trip up Vancouver Island to visit Nan and Pop Collins is just what the three need. Some space from the crazy ex-boyfriend and a break from the city. Not to mention, it's an excellent opportunity for Rebecca to finally meet Shamus and Claire. Excitement runs high as they prepare to leave, but so does the tension when Max declares he's in love with Rebecca.

While out in the country visiting, new dilemmas crop up, and the brothers still haven't smoothed out their earlier differences. Will these new challenges bring them closer together, or could this be what finally tears them apart for good?

Contracted To Mr. Collins Books One & Two

Hearing about an account executive position available at Collins Enterprises with a whopping $75,000 base salary, Rebecca D'Angelo immediately put together a stunning portfolio and marched downtown to apply. Finding herself on deadline and unsure of where to go, she darted toward the information desk. Stopped dead in her tracks, she thought for sure she had run into a brick wall.

Crashing to the floor, her latte and portfolio launch into the air. Her first thought, thankfully, she protected her documents with a plastic case. However, that abruptly changes when a set of large hands wrap around her arms and a deep rumbling voice echoes above her. "Jesus Christ! This is not a schoolyard, young lady!"
Looking up, her sight settles on a stunning 6'4" structure of a man that looks as if he just stepped off the cover of

a GQ Magazine. Suddenly, there's no mistaking who this man is — Aiden Collins, CEO of Collins Enterprises.

Just when she thinks all is lost, Rebecca makes it to the final round of interviews, but there's a catch. The last interview will be conducted by none other than Aiden Collins himself. Yep. Her dream job depends on the man she just ticked off.

The eye-opening experiences keep coming as the weeks turn into months. Rebecca quickly learns that Aiden has a twin brother Max and that they like to share their ladies. Oh, and her lifelong friends, she thought she knew and could trust – they start showing their true colours.

As the excitement unfolds, so do the dilemmas. Aiden may have fallen in love with her, but so did Max.

Adult situations and language 18+

Printed in Great Britain
by Amazon